T. W MacMahon

Cause and Contrast

An Essay on the American Crisis

T. W MacMahon

Cause and Contrast
An Essay on the American Crisis

ISBN/EAN: 9783337379674

Printed in Europe, USA, Canada, Australia, Japan

Cover: Foto ©Andreas Hilbeck / pixelio.de

More available books at **www.hansebooks.com**

CAUSE AND CONTRAST:

AN ESSAY

ON THE

AMERICAN CRISIS.

BY

T. W. MacMAHON.

RICHMOND, VA.
WEST & JOHNSTON.
1862.

CHAS. H. WYNNE, PRINTER.

TO

HIS EXCELLENCY,

JEFFERSON DAVIS;

FIRST PRESIDENT OF THE CONFEDERATE STATES:

SOLDIER, ORATOR, STATESMAN,

AND

CHOSEN CHIEF OF UNITED SOUTHERN PATRIOTISM;

WHO, IN VIOLATION OF

NO CONSTITUTIONAL OBLIGATION,

AND USURPING NO PRINCIPLE OF SPECIAL OR UNIVERSAL LIBERTY,

STANDS FORTH

A TRUE REPRESENTATIVE OF PURE AMERICANISM;

A GUARDIAN OF INDIVIDUAL RIGHTS;

AND

AN UPHOLDER OF

STATE SOVEREIGNTY:

This Essay

IS,

BY PERMISSION, RESPECTFULLY

DEDICATED.

PREFACE.

Early in the month of June last, or late in May, an editorial article appeared in the Charleston *Mercury*, recommending the production and encouragement of Southern literature, with which I was so forcibly impressed, as to resolve upon the composition and publication of the following essay. I felt that, at this crisis in our history, a brief work, containing a comprehensive and popularly written exposition of Southern political philosophy, might be advantageously placed before the world; and although there were far abler pens than mine in the land, upon which might have devolved this duty, their silence. impelled me to make the present attempt.

In my treatment of the subject, I have endeavored to be brief, lucid, and compendious—to make my little work as compact as possible, and spare the reader from useless or unnecessary reading. I have undertaken to prove historically, that slavery was originally a universal institution of all great governments and societies; but that the systems of the ancients were radically different from negro subordination in America. I have ventured to show that cannibalism and fetichism are, and ever have been, the normal and unalterable condition of the negro in his native home—that he is phy-

siologically and psychologically degraded, that he is of an inferior species of the human race, wholly dependent upon the Caucasian for progress, enlightenment, and well-being—and that,
servitude and subjection being his natural state, the relation
which he bears to superior mastership, in the Confederate
States, is merciful to him and the cause of religion and civilization.

Relative to the cruel sectional war into which we have been
plunged, I have, I think, established, that, so far as the
South is concerned, it was unavoidable—that it was forced
upon her against her will—in spite of her prayers and supplications.   The North was the first and original secessionist;
she rent asunder the old Union, and trampled under foot the
Constitution, which was the bond of Union; and, as such, let
her stand arraigned before the bar of posterity and universal
justice.

I do not claim anything like pure originality for this Essay.
Indeed, much of its matter may have been already familiar to
the reader.   But the style, arrangement, design, and mode of
treatment, are wholly my own.

I should not omit to mention here, that it has been my
good fortune to have recently become acquainted with a distinguished gentleman, whom I am proud to call my friend—
Hon. ALEXANDER DIMITRY. Of him I can truly add, that he
· is an accomplished critic, a profound thinker, and a fine
scholar—a man of Athenian acumen, and gifted with a
plastic Greek mind. I am indebted to him for important
suggestions, as well as for the reading and correcting of my
proof-sheets. To Professor DE BOW, whose fruitful labors have

peculiarly associated him with the industrial growth and development of the South, I am also obliged for kind attentions, and for having been instrumental in materially adding to my knowledge of cotton culture.

I must not, and should not, conclude, without offering sincere and unaffected thanks to my publishers—Messrs. WEST & JOHNSTON. They have promptly responded to every wish of mine, in the face of difficulties and expense, during the publication of this work. Indeed, Mr. Johnston, particularly,—Mr. West being absent in the military service of his country—has been to me, not only a business, but a personal, friend—always cheerful, courteous, generous and obliging; and if my *first* book meets with popular favor, it is merely designed to form, a general introduction to a history of the present war—which shall bear the imprint of my *first* publishers.

CONTENTS.

XVI.

XVII.

CAUSE AND CONTRAST.

"THE whole conduct of Cambyses," says Herodotus, the father of history, "towards the Egyptian gods, sanctuaries and priests, convinces me that this King was in the highest degree insane; for otherwise he would not have insulted the worship and holy things of a people." The coincidence between the conduct of Cambyses, one of the earliest rulers of men, and that of Mr. Abraham Lincoln, President of the United States of America, one of the latest rulers in Time, is singularly striking and remarkable. This King, Lincoln, has been, and now is, endeavoring to overthrow the institutions and ruin the prosperity of fifteen sovereign and independent Southern States: first, by insult, vilification, and contumelious abuse of their social system; then, by direct assault, or gradual encroachment upon their constitutional rights; and lastly, by seeking to slaughter their liberties beneath the iron heel of armed mercenary invaders. Instead of ruling in accordance with the eternal principles of rectitude and benevolence, he has chosen to inaugurate discord, hatred, and civil war, between thirty millions of brothers, and to convert a country smiling with loveliness and beauty, and teeming with wealth and prosperity, into a great Golgotha. He has violated that Constitution which he has sworn to observe and protect; he has made war without right or authority; he

1

has converted free institutions into instruments of despotism; he has prepared armed men for the sack and
carnage of great commercial cities, and the waste and
desolation of harvest fields—peaceful and happy homes;
and the Ocean, which should be the natural bond of
love and amity between the Nations, he has changed
into a high road of terror for the merchant, and a
barracks for his ships of war.

II.

THE historians of future ages, in philosophising upon
the unaccountable events of the past, will have to record
how the greatest and most favored country upon earth,
with the most liberal code of laws that the world had
yet witnessed, growing out of the rational theory of
individual self-government, was destroyed by the perverse fanaticism of a certain political organization, the
chosen chief of which is Abraham Lincoln. The ethics,
or doctrines rather, of this party are founded upon the
allegation, that negro subordination is contrary to Divine
law and revolting to the moral sense of mankind, and
that slavery is the creature of local or municipal codes
and at war with Nature. Such assumptions are untenable, fictitious, and iniquitous. And before passing over
to a review of that cruel question, which more immediately
destroys the peace and happiness of the American
people, we will proceed with a refutation of these fundamental errors: establishing that slavery is coeval with
the dawn of history and civilization, and existed antecedent to all written codes; showing that the subordination of the negro to the Caucasian is *not* slavery, but, that
being of physical and intellectual inferiority of organism,

this is his normal condition; and, finally, proving beyond cavil, that such a relation, in social economy, is wise, providential, and beneficent—having elevated the negro to a standard of civilization which he never attained before, and having furnished with labor millions of the superior race, and clothed more than one-half of civilized mankind.

III.

SLAVERY, at the commencement and formation of social and political societies, was universal as civilization; permanent as the free autonomy of nationalities; and constituted an integral element in the progress and greatness of the most remarkable governments that ever existed.   It was an Egyptian institution before the Pyramids were built or hieroglyphics invented; so in Syria and Assyria, before Babylon or Nineveh arose in splendor and beauty; and in Palestine long before Abraham first went into Egypt.   It was an institution of the Indians and the Chinese—of the Medes and Persians—of the Greeks and the Phœnicans—of the Romans and the several European nations; certainly as universal as law or order, and continuing down to the application, or substitution, of the mechanic arts for the performance of that brute labor formerly exacted of man.   And this economical and political element of order and civilization in society, was SLAVERY *per se—the subjection or constrained obedience of white men, made dependent upon rulers of the same caste and race with themselves:* but RADICALLY AND TOTALLY IN CONTRADISTINCTION TO THE SUBORDINATE RELATIONS OF THE NEGRO IN THE SOUTHERN STATES OF AMERICA.

It is not, however, our intention either to justify or condemn the systems of labor in other nations, no matter whether remote or immediate in time. To justify them would be to pronounce opinion from imperfect and superficial data; and to condemn, would be to set our dicta above the authority of the wisest and best men that ever lived—above the Divine Saviour—above Moses and the Patriarchs—Solon and Thrasybulus— Pythagoras and Socrates—Plato and Aristotle—Seneca and Cicero—Athanasius and Augustine. If ancient slavery, however, as is now alleged, was barbarism, it was inevitable; for it resulted from political and social exigencies, and the necessity of progressive life in public economy. The slaves who pastured flocks, herded cattle, and cultivated the soil, were, in return, protected from injury or invasion by their lords, standing ready with arms in their hands. The benefits and hardships of master and servant were then mutual. And now even, it would not be an uninteresting investigation to contrast this constrained labor of the ancients with the "voluntary" system of the moderns; clearly defining in what essential, other than mere form, they differ. Certain it is, that the boasted "freedom" of the modern operative is as much nominal as it is real; since the poor dependent of the present, by an instinct of self-preservation and family affection, is *compelled* to labor. He is free *not* to work, it is true; but not being a self-sustaining machine, he *must* do so or starve. Being a creature of Nature, he is subject to her laws and despotism. She teaches the birds of the air and the beasts of the forest, respectively, to nurture their young; and by a higher development of the emotional affections, she rules man in the same direction. He is her predestined slave, in proportion to the delicacy of his organism, and the refinement of his intellectual culture. Often poor and without means, he hires his services for a fixed remuneration, with which to purchase nourishment either for his parents or his offspring, or both; considerations which devolved as imperative duty upon the masters of antiquity. And thus the toiler of to-day is in *reality* a slave; differing only in appearance and degree from his brother-slave of other systems and ages past.

IV.

AT this remote period of time, and more especially in a brief and cursory view of the facts, it will be found impossible to present either a full or minute account of the relations which existed between master and slave in ancient nations. What we can derive from her hieroglyphic characters, and the paintings upon her tombs and monuments, is the principal means through which we can glance at Egypt's early domestic economy. The preponderance of Egyptian slaves was either purchased from barbarous nations or conquered in war. We behold in one place the king putting them to flight. In another, we see an officer registering and arranging them into separate classes—adults, women and minors. That they were generally foreigners we know, from the fact that it was the boast of the Pharaohs, that in the erection of the Pyramids and public monuments no Egyptian hands were employed. And GESCHE (the *Goshen* of the Bible), of which Heliopolis was the capital, and Moses one of the priests, was the district allotted to the Israelitish bondsmen and their families. The slaves of Egypt were employed in all occupations, agrestic and domestic; nor do they seem to have been cruelly treated; although the master, mistress and overseer are generally represented as wielding the lash while superintending them. This instrument, however, should be regarded in the unexpressive language of pictorial history, merely as the insignia of authority. For, on the contrary, upon a monument of Thebes, there is a picture copied by Sir Gardner Wilkinson, representing a lady enjoying the luxury of the bath and attended by four female slaves; where kindness on the part of the former, and respectful affection on that of the latter, are clearly delineated. And when the Jews planned their escape from the land of bondage to the land of promise, did they not succeed by false representations, in *borrowing* from their Egyptian masters precious vessels, jewelry and gold? That system, if unjust, could not have been very cruel, under which the master *lent* valuables toward the gratification of his cunning slave.

But these very Jews, at the time that they were transferred from their home into Egypt, and indeed long before this term of their captivity, were slaveholders themselves. And when they returned from bondage under Nehemiah, one-sixth of the people were at once slaves and captives. Abraham had his male slaves and female slaves; and Sarah was the tyrannical and cruel mistress of Hagar. When Rebecca married Isaac she carried to his home her slave-damsels; as did Leah, the wife of Laban, and Rachel, the spouse of Jacob. The Jews reduced the Gibeonites to "hewers of wood and drawers of water;" and whilst the *Hebrew* slave (unless he selected the contrary) was entitled to release at the year of Jubilee, and to be treated during his bondage as "a servant and sojourner," the *heathen* and the *stran-*

ger, on the other hand, became not only "a bond-man forever," but the "possession" and "the money" of his master and owner. Even Solomon, reputed to have been the wisest of men, a son of David (who was a man according to God's heart) and a direct ancestor of Christ —according to Matthew, the Evangelist—was, if judged by our modern international law, a common pirate; for his ships on the sea of Tarsus exported all sorts of merchandise to exchange for "ivory, *apes and Ethiopians.*" And when the Saviour of Mankind was upon earth, inculcating lessons of wisdom in the alleys and dark ways, on the mountains and highways, he not only acquiesced in, but approved of, such institutions, and healed the Centurion's slave; even as the apostle Paul returned to his Christian master the fugitive, Onesimus.

But we feel that it is unnecessary to dwell farther upon this subject. The question of Hebrew slavery has recently been fully and thoroughly examined by the Rev. Dr. Van Dyke, of Brooklyn, N. Y., and by the Rabbi Raphall* of New York city; each of them, in an elo-

---

* The influence exercised by abolitionism upon the best minds of the North, is peculiarly mournful. The "Bible View of Slavery," a sermon preached by Dr. Raphall, on the day of National fast, Jan. 4, 1861, is certainly the most scholarly and conclusive discourse written by any divine of his section. Yet, after invoking "the Father of Truth and Mercy to enlighten his mind," in his terror of the anti-slavery Moloch, he utters strange blasphemy. "My friends," says the sapient Rabbi, "I find, and *I am sorry* to find, that I am delivering a pro-slavery discourse. I am no friend to slavery in the abstract, and still less friendly to the practical workings of slavery. But I stand here as *a teacher in Israel;* not to place before you my own feelings and opinions, but to propound to you THE WORD of GOD, the *Bible View of Slavery.*" A Tammany politician would scorn to stultify himself thus. The Doctor absolutely sets his own wisdom above that

quent sermon, clearly maintaining that the Jews did not regard slavery as contrary to the laws of Nature or of Nature's God. And, indeed, their task was easy and incontrovertible, since, in addition to the old Jewish common law, the laws given by Moses to the Jews were drawn from the Egyptian system of polity, but purified by the Hebrew Theogony.

V.

SLAVERY assumed in India a religious as well as a political character. The labors of the slave were lightened and alleviated by a spiritual resignation of Faith. He believed that at the creation, although sprung from the Deity, his condition of life was immutably fixed. All men, according to Menu, are divided into four classes; the first of which sprang from the mouth of God and are gifted to rule and to sacrifice. The second, born of His arm, are endued with the strength to fight in defence of the other classes. The third, or the children of His abdomen are allotted to agriculture, traffic and trade. The fourth were the offspring of His feet, and naturally doomed to *servitude*. But this predestination of the latter does not seem to have been regretted; for to serve a Brahmin was esteemed both laudable and honorable. Aside from this classification, however, there was a Hindoo code under which slaves were made by voluntary sale; by sale of children; by servile birth; by marriage to a slave; by sale for debt; and by captivity in war.

---

of God. Like an obedient, but hypocritical servant, he preaches abroad the word and will of his Master; but he "is sorry" for doing it! Is not this Abolition blasphemy?

So, also, were persons committing crimes against nature or society (entailing forfeiture of life in other nations), reduced to slavery. This continued until Mohammedanism predominated, and, as usual with that power, introduced its own innovations; recognizing but two sources of slavery—captive infidels and their descendants. Such slaves were subject to all the laws of sale and inheritance. They could not marry without permission from their masters; nor be parties to a suit; nor bear testimony in Courts of Justice; nor inherit or acquire property; nor be eligible to any office of trust or emolument. But in 1793, British power, through the agency of the East India Company, modified all this, declaring that "Mohammedan law, with reference to Mohammedans, and Hindoo law with reference to Hindoos," were henceforward to be regarded as the general rules of Indian jurisprudence; thus recognizing by one enactment two systems of slavery in the same country.

VI.

It would be difficult to name a people, no matter of what ethnic origin or affinity, who were not slave-owners; and with whom slavery was not one of the earliest institutions. It seems to have been the natural relation of the weak to the powerful—of the captive to the conqueror—of the dependent to the opulent. It is doubtful whether it was ever founded upon any statutory enactments, but existed rather by prescription; since its origin was antecedent to history or tradition. Thus: It is almost certain, and if not quite certain, decidedly probable, that the primitive inhabitants of Susiana—Elamites, doubtless—were conquered by Hamites and reduced to a condition

of servitude.   This Hamite race wrested Babylonia from
the Median Scyths—a mixture of Japhetic and Turaunian
races—twenty-three centuries before Christ.   According
to Berosus, after a reign of 258 years, these Hamite
conquerors were in turn superseded in power by emigrants
from Susiana—the founders of the great Chaldean Empire.   The captives, as usual, became the servants of the
conquerors.   It was at this period that the Exodus of
Abraham took place—when the Hebrew patriarch, with
his household, marched from Chaldea to Palestine—and
when the Phœnicans emigrated from the Persian Gulf
to the shores of the Mediterranean; each carrying with
them the precious institution of slavery.   It was at
this period that Semitic tribes displaced the Cushite
inhabitants of the Arabian peninsula; that Assyria was
becoming occupied by the Semitic settlers of Babylonia;
and that the eastern frontier of Syria was in course of
occupation by Aramæans—*all and each of whom had
slaves and slavery*.   And when Arabian supremacy was
established in the Chaldean Empire, no less than when
the seat of empire, in the 13th century B. C., was again
transferred to Assyria—amid all vicissitudes of time, and
war, and change, slavery continued the same; no matter
what people or race might rule.

The autonomy of the latter, and the greater Assyrian
Empire, continued at least during six centuries; and the
palaces and temples of Sardanapalus—the palace at
Nineveh of Shalmanubar; he of the Black Obelisk—the
palace of Sargon, at Khorsabad—the many and magnificent palaces of Esar-haddon; the wonderful hunting
palace of his successor—would be, (if we had not the
testimony of the Bible even to guide us,) no silent witnesses to the wisdom, extent, importance, utility, skill

ASSYRIAN SLAVERY.   11

and intelligence, of that system of labor which mainly contributed toward their execution. The slaves and captives whom it was unnecessary to employ upon the public works were colonized abroad. Thus the Chaldeans were sent into Armenia; the Jews and Israelites into Assyria and Media; and the Babylonians and Susianians, into Palestine. And yet these Assyrian slave-dealers and slave-owners—it will seem incredible to the unenlightened—were in all the elements of civilization and advancement, if we except a barbarous religion and savage passions, very nearly, if not completely, upon a par with our own boasted progress.

Out of the ruin of the Assyrian Empire, it was, that the later Babylonish Empire arose, in brilliant but brief splendor. When Saracus was betrayed by Nabopolassar, his General and the father of Nebuchadnezzar, Josiah, King of Judea, was tributary to the Assyrian; and in the division of the empire between Cyaxares, the Mede, and Nabopolassar, Judea, Syria, Phœnicia, &c., fell to the lot or choice of the latter. Nineveh, of course, was taken and destroyed; the bulk of the people became captives, and were equally divided. With these captives, remarkably advanced in a knowledge of the fine arts, and especially of architecture, it was, that Nabopolassar commenced the magnificent works which Nebuchadnezzar completed. When, however, the Egyptian king, Necho, made war upon the former, defeated Josiah and put his elder brother Jehoiakim upon the throne, Nebuchadnezzar went out against him and drove him back into Egypt. During his absence Nabopolassar died, and Nebuchadnezzar, followed by captive Jews, Phœnicans, Syrians and Egyptians, returned to assume the government. These captives he distributed over various parts of Babylon; the great number of which, however, when added to the prisoners of his father, gave him command of that power which enabled him to consummate those great works that were then among the wonders of the world, and the ruins of which excite the mingled awe and admiration of the present generation. With this slave labor he built the great *outer* wall which fortified his capital: it was 130 square miles, 80 feet wide, and from three to four hundred feet high—*embracing altogether about two hundred millions yards of solid masonry!* Inside of this, there was another wall of nearly equal importance. He had built in seventeen days' time a splendid palace, the ruins of which are still extant. He had built or rebuilt all the cities of upper Babylonia, and Babylon itself. He had dug immense canals; formed aqueducts; raised pyramidal temples and other sacred shrines; made immense reservoirs; built quays and breakwaters; and constructed the wonderful hanging-gardens of Babylon. But during the construction of these works, the Jews revolted three times; and in the reign of one of their kings, Zedekiah, Jerusalem was invested—destroyed—and the bulk of its inhabitants made to swell the captives of Nebuchadnezzar. With this immense additional servile population, he continued to embellish his capital, and to prosecute the construction of works for public utility. After a reign of forty-three years, Nebuchadnezzar died, leaving the crown to his son, Evil-Merodach. The successor of this prince witnessed, doubtless, the opening of that Revolution, which, by the overthrow of Astyages, established the great Persian Empire under Cyrus. At any rate one of his successors, Nabonadius, entered into alliance with Cræsus, the Lydian, which finally resulted in the capture of Babylon, then in charge of Belshazzar; for Nabonadous was at Borsippa. This latter city soon shared the fate of the capital, and with it the old Chaldean Empire fell under the dominion of the victorious Persian; and master and slave alike became the captive property of the victor.

Lydia first arose to importance under the reign of Gyges. It was, however, once previously invaded and overrun by the Cimmerians, who reduced a portion of the inhabitants to a condition of servitude. These Cimmerians were themselves fugitives that fled from before the more victorious Scyths, leaving many of their brethren behind in captivity. But during the reign of Sadyattes, the Cimmerian power in Lydia began to decline; and by Alyattes, his successor, they were either extirpated or reduced to slavery. A war of greater importance soon ensued; Alyattes became engaged with Cyaxares, the Mede, by whom Lydia was invaded. The war continued six years with doubtful issue; but always resulting in slavery to the respective captives. At length an eclipse—supposed to have been that of Thales—put an end to the war; and Alyattes spent the remainder of his reign in peace, or in the erection of his mammoth sepulchre—equal in grandeur to the best Egyptian pyramid—by the hands of his captives and "the tradesmen, handicraftsmen, and courtezans of Sardis."

The conclusion of this war between the contending powers, was also the commencement of a strict alliance between the Lydians and the Medes. The latter was a branch of the great Arian family, and closely allied in language and lineage to the Persians. Their manners and customs, and still more their institutions, were not radically dissimilar. The Medes under Cyaxares, it is plausibly conjectured, commenced their migration by issuing from Khorasan; passing along the mountain chain south of the Caspian Sea; entering Media; conquering the Scyths; blending with a portion of them, reducing others to servitude, and precipitating the untractable upon the Assyrians; which, finally, resulted in the overthrow and destruction of the empire of the latter. Within eight or nine years of the establishment of his power in Media, Cyaxares was master of Nineveh. In this enterprise he was assisted, as we have seen, by the traitorous General of Saracus, Nabopolassar. Babylon became not only sovereign and independent, but aggressive and conquering—always in alliance with Media; and, by the peace of the latter with Lydia, a triple alliance followed, embracing the Babylonish power. This alliance was cemented by royal intermarriages, and lasted about fifty years. The allied kingdoms, however, continued respectively to absorb some lesser surrounding powers, and to reduce their inhabitants to servitude. At length the Persian irruption under Cyrus came. Babylon was leveled with the dust, and the pride of her allies subdued. Again the proud masters of Babylonia, Media and Lydia, in the uncertainty and vicissitudes of the times, became the captives of the Persian—the slaves, in fact, of the conquering Pasargadæ, Maraphii, and Achæmenidæ; for with them, as with all other dominant races, slavery was a civil and religious institution.

Thus we see, that during the greatest period of the world's history, so long dim and obscure to human knowledge, and only partially and imperfectly revealed to us now, by the light of modern research and criticism, *Slavery was the invariable and universal superstructure of all social and political systems.* ·

VII.

THE ground over which we have hitherto trodden, has been, until recently, deemed pre-historic; but now we are to enter that plastic region, where the light of history first begins to grandly shine—where man reached his highest development—

> "Where grew the arts of war and peace,
> Where Delos rose and Phœbus sprung;"—

the renowned and lovely classic soil of Greece. Yet is the morning of her history but dimly revealed to us by her poetry and myths. Her noble songs and unrivalled epics and dramas are her earliest histories. Her poets—inspired men, who stood forth to reveal the past, to explain the present, and to make known the future—were her original historians. And their theme was usually divinely exalted—their gaze attracted by the heroic legend and the splendid action, rather than by the petty transactions of slaves; excepting when it became necessary to illustrate noble deeds by little ones. Hence it is difficult to always arrive at a correct idea of the early economy of her little States.

In Greece lots of arable land were parcelled out to certain individuals, with carefully marked and jealously watched boundaries; but the greater portion of the country was devoted to pasturage. Cattle formed the main item of wealth. These were tended by bought slaves or poor hired freemen, called in Attica, Thêtes. The slaves upon whom this trust devolved were generally high in the confidence of their masters; Eumæus, the swine-herd of Ulysses, and himself the son of a king, being doubtless a fair type of his class. Indeed, these slaves had often under their control, as auxiliaries, subordinate slaves, who were treated in a manner neither harsh nor cruel. Their condition was little, if at all, worse than that of the Thêtes; who, nominally free, but owning no land, wandered about from one temporary job to another; generally contented if during the harvest or other busy seasons they could give their labor in exchange for food and clothing; and not unfrequently bartering away their freedom for the more permanent and secure protection of a master.

The Constitution of Sparta—and especially the Code of Lycurgus—rendered slavery an absolute necessity to the State. By this Code all distinction of rank as between Spartan *citizens* was abolished. The design of the great law-giver was to elevate rather than depress his fellow-countrymen. Lacedæmonians, politically considered, were to be regarded upon a footing of perfect and complete equality; they were to be as members of one family—as children of the same roof. The exercise of mechanism, or even of agriculture, was imperatively prohibited to the free. Every Lacedæmonian was required to live up strictly to the standard of a modern nobleman or aristocrat, and to cultivate the spirit of chivalry and patriotism. Hence, slaves and slavery became necessary, general, and numerous. The Helotism of Sparta, however, seems to have been the severest system of ancient involuntary labor. It was peculiarly marked out for censure by many able Athenians; and its evils not only grossly exaggerated, but shamefully misrepresented. It would be difficult, indeed, to name another rustic population which enjoyed greater immunities than the Spartan Helots. Their hearths were inviolate. Their social intercourse was free. They had a fixed and moderate rent-scale. They might acquire property by industrious exertions. And, were it not for the institution of the *Krypteia*—the existence of which is uncertain and doubtful—their condition was much superior to that enjoyed at the present day by the down-trodden peasantry of Europe.

Wherever the Ionians or Dorians—the two great branches of the Greek family—colonized, they carried along with them the parent institution of slavery. Thus, the Argives and slaves whom they denominated *Gymnesii*, and resembling in their condition the helots of Sparta. The *Konipodes*, or dusty feet, of the Epidaurians, were a similar class. Regular slavery, upon the basis of the Athenian constitution, prevailed at Corinth and the *Corynephori* were the bondsmen of Sycion. In Crete—Crete of the "hundred cities"—there were two kinds of slaves—slaves that were the property of the State, and slaves that belonged to private individuals. In Syracuse their number was proverbial, and their labor caused the estates of the nobles to yield the richest harvests and to blossom like the rose. Megara had her slaves and slave constitution; and the Megarian colony of Byzantium placed the Bithynians in a condition of Helotism. The Mariandynians were similarly held by the Heracleans; and Thera, with her colony of Cyrene, clung to the old Doric usage. Tarentum, the city of Archytes, a virtuous Pythagorean, had her slaves and slave laws; and Crotona, the home of Pythagoras—the great political work of his brain being her constitution—was precisely in the same relation. All of these constituted the colonial glory of the Doric, and partially of the Ionic races. They, like the parent States, were great in

2

war, great in peace, great in commerce, great in literature and the fine arts, great in architecture; matchless
in every intellectual development which advances prosperity, civilization, and the glory of a people. They
flourished and progressed through their own virtue and
excellent institutions, including that of slavery; which
was among the primal elements of their happiness and
security.

Yet it has been confidently asserted upon the floor of
the United States Senate, and upon the authority of one
Gurowski, an itinerant Russian, that "slavery was the
putrescent mass which ruined Greece." The early vocation, and limited advantages of the Senator who retailed
this bold error, constitute the best apology for his ignorance. "The Grecian States," says K. O. Müller—an
author to whose profound erudition, great labors, and
critical perspicacity, universal scholarship is infinitely
indebted—"either contained a class of bondsmen, which
can be traced in nearly all the Doric States, or they had
slaves, who had been brought either by captivity or
commerce from barbarous countries; or a class of slaves
was altogether wanting, as was the case with the Pho-
cians and Locrians. *But these nations, scanty in resources, never attained to such grandeur and power as
Sparta and Athens.* SLAVERY WAS THE BASIS OF THE
PROSPERITY OF ALL COMMERCIAL STATES, AND WAS IN-
TIMATELY CONNECTED WITH FOREIGN TRADE." When
Athens was at the zenith of her glory and power, she
had only a population of 30,000 freemen, while her slave
population was over 400,000. Her fall resulted from
political demagogueism, perfidy and treachery. And, indeed, the decline and ruin of all Greek States are traced
to similar causes—the factious contentions of heartless

politicians, who divided and distracted the people by means of dangerous and glittering abstractions. With the virtue and greatness of Greece, the institution of slavery was fostered and prospered; but when the philosophy of Socrates, Plato and Aristotle—advocates of slavery—was forgotten; when the moral political examples of Solon, Aristides, and Pericles, were superseded, by the political *expediencies* of professional time-servers, tricksters, and place-hunters, Greece sank from liberty, splendor, and glory, into decrepitude, chains and ruin.

VIII.

As with early Greece, so with early Rome;—her social and economical history is shrouded from our penetration in the thick haze of myths, poetry, and tradition. But this much is clear: that from the very foundation of her society—coeval with the regulation of family relations—and long before the birth of her poets and historians, slavery was one of Rome's most valued institutions; and continued so, not only until the Cross was erected upon the ruins of Paganism, but long after the sceptre of Rome had passed beneath the triumphant banner of the stranger and barbarian. Indeed, the immutable principles of justice were so clearly discerned by the inflexible rectitude of the Roman mind, and so sagaciously applied by the wisdom of Roman lawyers, that Christianity, when supreme even in the Empire, approvingly adopted the old Roman statutes. That sacred religion, whose sanctity was sealed by the death of the noblest martyrs, and whose triumph sprang from their blood, naturalized as its own civil ethics, the provisions of the Roman slave code; founded as they were upon the experience and accumu-

lated wisdom of ages. Throughout the "Code" of
Justinian there is a full recognition of slavery—a broad
and unquestionable distinction made between the free
and the servile—and by the acknowledged disqualifica-
tion for freedom of those who were captured in war; of
those who sold themselves or were legally sold into
slavery; and of those who were of servile descent—a
virtual denial of natural equality.* Antoninus placed
the life of the slave within the protection of the law: the
Christian emperor did no more, but candidly ascribed
this boon even to his pagan predecessor. He ratified
the law of Constantine, which made it homicide to
maliciously kill a slave; and he confirmed the law of
Claudius against the abandonment of sick and useless
slaves. And whatever amelioration was effected in the
condition of the slave under the laws of Justinian, resulted from a spirit of policy in public economy—as they

---

* Professor Taylor Lewis, in his "reply" to a sermon of Dr. Van
Dyke, noticed already in the text, rises to the sublime of ignorance.
"The Roman servitude was bitter enough," says he, "but still with
hope [false cant! the Roman slave had no *right* to 'hope;' in this
respect he was not upon a level with the negro slave] remaining at the
bottom. Emancipation might speedily restore the *doulos*, [This, Professor, was a *Greek* and *not* a Roman slave, and 'emancipation' is as
much the privilege of the negro as it was of either the Roman *servus*
or Greek doulos,] or his children, to the level of society. It was,
therefore, a better thing (sic) than this Calhoun, (!) Hamitic [This is
a mere theological fancy, and not scholarship or erudition, Professor,]
bondage, 'normal,' endless, hopeless, to which no year of jubilee
[Surely, Professor, *you ought to know* that you now tread upon Hebrew
and not upon Roman ground,] shall ever come."

Now, this is one of the oracles of Northern ignorance. He passes
for a great man in New York. We have quoted from him but three
sentences; and behold the confusion of facts and ideas! When the
blind lead the blind, both will fall into the pit.

expressly set forth—rather than from any promptings of
what is now termed evangelical humanity. The *life* of
the slave was protected, but his political inferiority
sternly fixed and asserted. A free person could not wed
a slave; and this distinction was fully recognized, nay,
but sanctified, by Christianity—the Church steadfastly
and persistently refusing its blessings to such unions.
But the Church went still further. A fugitive slave,
desirous of becoming a monk, could be reclaimed by his
master at any time during his three years of probation.
Leo the Great opposed the promotion of slaves to the
dignity of the sacerdotal office; because that the Church
might thereby become a refuge for contumacious slaves,
and invade the rights of property; and because such
accessions brought discredit upon the Clergy. In all
cases the consent of the master was an imperative necessity. But a measure of general enfranchisement was
never contemplated by the greatest and wisest of Christian writers, philosophers, law-givers and saints. The
trade in slaves was a principal and recognized branch of
commerce. Man was marketable; and he so continued,
until the decay and decrepitude of the Roman power,
failed to supply the markets with hordes of conquered
barbarians—until Roman glory was crushed beneath the
savage heel of Vandal, Goth, Lombard, Gaul and
Hun. Long after this, as we shall soon see, the laws in
relation to slavery continued to be the same in effect as
in the previous past. Basil, the Macedonian, was among
the first to interpose on behalf of the bond—claiming
that the union of a slave with a free person ought to be
sealed by the Christian sacrament of matrimony; but
more than four centuries elapsed before the Christian
Church universally conceded what Basil advocated: for

in the thirteenth century, we find Nicetus, Bishop of Thessalonica, excommunicating masters who refused their slaves the privilege of being married in the Church.

IX.

UPON the ruin of the Roman Empire the power and dominion of the Barbarian arose. That Empire once comprehended the largest and fairest portion of the earth. But when Theodoric, the Ostrogoth, was crowned King of Italy, the glory of the Empire may be said to have passed away. Roman dominion, indeed, still prevailed; but only in a religious sense. The Western World was rapidly becoming Christian and Catholic. The bishops and missionaries of the Church were all, or nearly all, of the Latin race, and spoke the Latin tongue. They stood between the rude barbarian and an angry and exacting Deity, as mediators and intercessors—they were regarded as the commissioned advocates of the sinner and the transgressor—men of delegated holiness, whose prayers ascended daily before Seraphim and Cherubim. It was natural that these cultivated men, the sole depositaries of the learning of the times, and the only advance guard of Civilization and Christian humanitarianism, should become the teachers of barbarians and the moulders of their actions. And the spirit of Christianity rendered them bold, fearless and generous. As Agapetus confronted the Emperor Justinian and his courtezan queen—as Silverius defied the frowns, threats and persecutions of Belisarius and his lewd wife, Antonina—and as Pelagius I. stood undismayed before Totila—so did many of these soldiers of the Christian cross peril their lives in the cause of humanity and civilization,—precipitating themselves between savage men and their victims, until by sacred lesson and example they changed or modified the passions of the barbarians. They became the reconcilers of hostile races and the harmonizers of different laws and customs. For the Barbaric codes, like the Roman law, recognized slavery as the ordinary, if not the normal, condition of a portion of mankind. With them, as with the Romans, man was merchandise. But, happily for mankind, the captive in war did not forfeit his life, but his liberty, by defeat; otherwise the wars of the whole world must have been wars of massacre and extermination. The clergy interposed their benign religious influence on behalf of the unfortunate, and soothed or ameliorated their condition by overawing the cruel. But the system of slavery, in all its legal essentials, remained the same. It was too permanently and too universally rooted—too firmly founded upon principles of justice, social, religious and philanthropic necessity—to admit of radical change or perceptible disturbance. The capture and sale of men was a principal branch of commerce along all the shores of Europe. Clovis encouraged the sale of the Alemanni; Charlemagne that of the Saxons, and Henry the Fowler that of the *sclaves*—captives from whose ethnic name we derive the term *slave*. Even when the slave was a Christian, if his domestic or family relations were secured or respected by law or usage, the boon was due to religion rather than to any theory of personal rights or humanity. The Lombards acknowledged the sanctity of the marriage contract between slaves; but marriage between those belonging to different owners was strictly prohibited; and by the Salic law, the slave who married without consent of his master was punished

by an hundred stripes and a specified mulct. Nearly all
the Barbarian codes, like the Roman, prohibited the debasing alliance of free persons with slaves. By the Salic
and Ripuarian laws, the freeman who married a slave,
forfeited his freedom; and where a free woman married
a slave, both were, by the Lombard and Burgundian
statutes, condemned to death. The Visigothic code consigned to death the freewomen who married, or even had
intercourse, with her slave. The Saxon laws declared
the like penalty not only against free persons marrying
slaves, but even against those who married persons of
inferior rank. Unlike the Roman, the Barbaric codes
protected the *person* of the slave *because* he was *property*. All injury done to him was an injury to property
rather than to person; and the master, not the sufferer,
received the compensation. The edict of Theodoric provided that the murderer of another's slave should furnish
the injured master with two slaves instead. Indeed, the
power of life and death was in the master's hands;
since, according to the codes, he had a perfect right to
do away with his own property. The Latin Church
zealously labored to reform this savage abuse, by endeavoring to have the Hebrew code, or the more humane
edicts of Antoninus, Claudius and Justinian, engrafted
upon the barbaric laws. And hence (although the right
of life and death over a slave was the unquestioned usage
of all German tribes from times immemorial) we find the
provisions of the Mosaic law embodied in the Capitu-
laries of Charlemagne; while, under Lothaire, the murderer of a slave was punished by penance and excommu-
nication. The fugitive from labor and servitude became
an Ishmael on the face of the earth. It was criminal to
conceal him. As by our own common law the owner of

property may recover it wherever he finds it, so the master might seize his slave anywhere, and punish him according to pleasure. The churches and the monasteries were large slaveholders; and to harbor or conceal the runaway slave of an ecclesiastic was doubly criminal. Yet fortunate was the fugitive that succeeded in seeking refuge at the altar. Before he was restored, a promise was exacted from the master to remit all punishment. When we add that the Anglo-Saxon Abbott, Alcuin, owned ten thousand slaves, some correct idea may be formed of the extent of ecclesiastical property in slaves. The countrymen of Alcuin furnished the slave market with many of the most precious specimens of that kind of merchandise. The beauty of some Anglo-Saxons, exhibited in the Roman slave mart, excited the compassion of Gregory the Great, and led to their conversion by the great missionary, Saint Augustine. The Irish bought Anglo-Saxon slaves extensively, but manumitted them by a decree of a National Council in 1172—a principle of generous humanity, which England long afterward rewarded, by conquering and enslaving Ireland. The people of Northumberland sold their nearest relatives, often—according to the venerable Bede and William of Malmesbury—their very children. But with the sway of William the Conqueror came Norman vassalage—when the native master and slave were alike compelled to do homage to new lords. At length, but slowly and gradually, the influence of the Latin Church—the amalgamation of races—the relations of different races to each other, growing out of conquest, intercourse and change of dynasties—the final establishment of the European political system—the attachment of the slave to the soil in the character of serf—and the change in the laws which rendered slaves taxable property, and, therefore, a source of oppression and expense; all these influences, together with the advances made in the discovery and application of the mechanic arts, modified the relations of master and servant. Slavery became villeinage. Yet their condition was one not much improved by this change. In some cases, villeins might still be sold like cattle. In other instances, they could only be sold with the freehold. They could not always purchase their own liberty. The child followed the condition of the father. Like all other species of property, they were inheritable. They could not be admitted as witnesses in courts of justice. The runaway could be recovered by his master in the same manner as he would recover his horse or his ass. But the lord had not the power of life or limb over his vassal or serf. And when Henry VIII. and his characteristic daughter, Queen Elizabeth, commenced the work of manumission or emancipation, they did so through no philanthropic or religious motive, but simply to replenish their empty treasuries, *by selling freedom to their enslaved vassals.* Another reason was, that towards the close of the reign of Elizabeth, the utility of the negro was discovered; and it is to this discovery that Enlgand is largely indebted for her present commercial wealth and ascendancy, as well as for the abolition of villeinage. Upon the negro question we shall soon enter; but whether—if we accept the securities conceded to his rights of person—the condition of the Caucasian vassal has been improved by his enfranchisement may well admit of some doubt.

One country—one people rather—remain to be spoken of—the Moslems. Long before Mohammed was born, slavery was in full force in distracted and divided Arabia—under all of her petty kings and chiefs. But united by Islamism—when the prophet of Allah gave to her the laws of Divine revelation—slavery became firmly fixed, perpetual and sanctified. It was one of the ordinary conditions of society, and it so continues to the present day. The Koran is, when regarded in its religious authoritativeness amongst the people, an eternal edict of servitude. At the time, however, that Mohammed lived, wrote and fought, slavery was an universal institution; founded upon the principles of universal laws; and hence, in the wars of Christian against Moor, many centuries afterward, which were inspired by dogmatic zeal, the system became not only increased, but debased. France and Italy were filled with Saracen slaves. In turn, the Saracen markets were overflowing with Christian captives, offered for sale by Jewish traders. And this example was copied during the German and Slavonic wars. So, Venetian ships were the carriers of slaves; slavery existed in Poland while Poland had life; and when nationally dead, Russia—where serfdom existed from the foundation of the Muscovite Empire—revived the system upon her corpse.

X.

It was not a sentiment of doctrinal or moral humanity which impelled the masters and owners of men to emancipate the slaves of their own race and lineage. For while villeinage prevailed in England—while feudalism, the maxims of the old Saxon Constitution, and Danish and Norman customs, were yet the law of the land, the Church, her holy fathers, monks and friars—according to the secretary of Edward VI., Sir Thomas Smith—

interposed at the confessional, and in the ministry of extreme unction, for the amelioration of the condition of the servile. But on behalf of whom did these holy men so interpose? Was it for a heterogeneous race? Was it in the cause of savages or unreclaimed heathens? Was it on behalf of a people morally and physically repulsive, and intellectually degraded and inferior, whose normal and characteristic condition was that of servitude and subordination? No. It was on behalf of Englishmen who were of the same caste and race with their masters—descendants of Britons, Danes, Saxons, Angles, Picts and Normans—men who were of the same complexion and anatomical structure as their lords, and in whose veins coursed the kindred blood of a kindred lineage—men whose only inferiority was artificial and accidental, resulting from inherited poverty—and men whose progeny were destined in time to develop the most brilliant intellectual faculties in every department that sheds glory, or fame, or immortality, around intellectual life. Yet when emancipation gradually, but systematically commenced, it was founded upon principles of political economy purely. As we have seen, the monarchs sold freedom to their vassals. In the possession of the lord they were taxable property, and, consequently, a source of enormous expense. Philosophy and mechanism were advancing; the policy and necessity of exacting brute labor from man was receding. Each new discovery in science and the mechanic arts gave a fresh impetus to the progress and elevation of the serf, until at length the ethics of public economy found the ingenious susceptibilities, refined mental organism, and inventive genius of the Caucasian, more profitable in guiding the helm of the ship and directing the steam engine through the tunnel and down the rapid grade, than in rudely squandering away his power in a patriarchal manner, whereby the fruit of his labor would sink into comparative infinitesimal insignificance. The Sun of Civilization was rapidly reaching its meridian orbit. The progress made in useful inventions was considerable. The Spanish armada was destroyed. The Dutch broom was soon to be swept from the English channel. Bacon was writing his *Novum Organum.* Shakespeare was producing his noblest tragedies. Soon the *Principia* of Newton would produce a revolution in mathematics and astronomy. The Spirit of the Age was marching forward—onward rolled the wheels of progress. A few more years, and the Caucasian will remove the burden from off the shoulders of his brother—the steam engine will perform the labor of a million of toilers—the reaping machine will substitute the harvest hand in the harvest field—the cotton-gin and cotton jenny will daily do the work of hundreds—the sewing machine will strip of half its tragic pathos the "Song of the Shirt"—and international codes will loose their former stern aspect, and appear more gentle and benign. No more shall the captive in war remain the captor's slave; because equality of intellect and race among the peoples of Europe must become a recognized fact of international law; and because the improvement made in war engines and instruments of destruction renders the chances of war alike equal and uncertain. It will no more appear wise or rational to retain and support a captured enemy upon an already over-populated soil. Public and political economy alike forbid it.

Nevertheless, the physical condition of the European hirelings and servants of the present day, is but little,

if anything, in advance of that of the ancient Villein.
Many of them, ragged or barefoot, toil daily for a pittance, not sufficient to provide their half-starved and half-
famished families with the scantiest and coarsest food.
Circumstances have altered, indeed, the relation of master and servant; but the nature and characteristics of
the task-master are still the same. The distance of sympathy, mutual dependence and kindliness, which separates the cotton-spinners of New England and the iron
masters of Pennsylvania, from their operatives, is as
great as that which separates the lord from his vassal—
INFINITELY greater than that which separates the Southern planter from his negro slave. And it is quite
natural that this should be so. Property is precious.
It is better and cheaper for the employer to hire for a
pittance the daily laborer, than risk the life of his valuable slave in the performance of menial or dangerous
service. Hence we find the Roman freemen; the Athenian Thêtes, the Spartan Perioïkoi, frequently exchang-
ing their liberties for the protection and security of a
master. And, indeed, fortunate would it be for the
wretched operatives of the manufacturing towns of. England; the coal-miners of Cornwall; and the stone-
breaking, ditch-digging, dung-carrying, half-starved,
semi-nude, bare-headed, and bare-footed peasantry of
Ireland, if such a source of refuge were still left open to
them. But no: the condition of the modern laborer
differs only in degree, not in effect, from that of the
vassal or the slave. He is still a craven dependent.
And whatever little advantages he may possess, are the
fruits of science and philosophy, rather than of religion
or philanthropy in the heart of his master. This will,
and indeed must, continue so, until labor is placed, if it

ever can be, upon a level with capital. Perhaps, by the observation of particular facts in the general law of physics, some future evangel of science may discover some principle of mechanism, that will place the toiler, socially and politically, upon an equality with the capitalist; but until that day arrives, surely the Caucasian has room enough to exercise his philanthropy on behalf of his crushed and down-trodden brother, without Quixotically spending his power and his pity on the side of that marked and debased slave of nature and circumstances—the *negro*.

Yet this is one of the crying errors of the present generation of would-be liberators and philanthropists. They build their arguments upon the false thesis, that *all* species of mankind had a common origin; and, indeed, were or are the children and lineal descendants of a single pair.* Because the Roman patriot who assas-

---

* "But all this," the superficial thinker will exclaim, "is contrary to the Mosaic account." He must really pardon us for differing from him: we are no less Christian than he. Moses never intended to have the negro regarded as a child of Adam and Eve. The Mosaic view of our first parents, their aspect and characteristics, is our view; and is fully and sublimely expressed by the inspired Christian poet—Milton:

> "Two of far nobler shape, erect and tall,
> God-like erect, in native honor clad
> In naked majesty, seemed lords of all,
> And worthy seemed: for in their looks divine
> *The image of their glorious Maker shone,*
> Truth, wisdom, sanctitude divine and pure,
> Severe, but in true filial freedom placed;
> Whence true authority in man; though both
> Not equal, as their sex not equal, seemed;
> For contemplation he and valor formed,
> For softness she and sweet attractive grace;
> He for God only, and she for God in him.
> *His fair large front and eye sublime declared*

sinated Cæsar for his royal aspirations, could sacrifice a
legion of gladiators for dreaming of freedom—because
the Saxon conqueror who boasted of Hampden, Sydney,
and Locke, could ruthlessly and unscrupulously trample
under foot the liberties of an Irish Celt—it has, by
arguments which were hoped to appear analogous, been
held equally wrong, oppressive, and tyrannical, in the
Virginia planter, whose chief pride it is that he lives
under a free constitution, to hold his African servant in
subjection.   But Lord Macaulay—who so reasoned—
should not have forgotten that the Gladiator and the Celt
were equally with their masters children of Caucasian
parents—that in their veins flowed the pure blood of a
superior race—that it was by the laws of captivity or
conquest, rather than of conceded degradation and inferiority, that they were held in subordination—and that
they respectively belonged to as brilliant and creative
branches of the great Arian family as any that migrated
westward from the uplands of India.   It is to the families of this Arian race—Scyths, Gauls, Franks, and
Germans—from which the Gladiators of the Roman
amphitheatre were drawn, (and from which the Capuan
Spartacus, was a fair type), that we are largely indebted

Absolute rule; and *hyacinthine locks*
Round from his parted forelock manly hung
Clustering, but not beneath his shoulders broad:
She, as a veil, *down to the slender waist*
Her unadorned golden tresses wore
Dishevelled, but in wanton ringlets waved
As the vine curls her tendrils."

Now let the reader imagine, if he can conceive, this as a picture of
a negro Adam and Eve; or let him show how a negro race could pos-
sibly spring from such parentage. But the reason and philosophy of
this question will be hereafter made apparent in the text.

for much of all that is sublime and beautiful in poetry and the plastic arts—in our Gothic architecture and Gothic civilization. The contributions of the Irish branch of the Celtic family to history, are no less famous. The Senate of no other nation could boast of more illustrious statesmen than Burke, Grattan, Canning, Sheridan, and Palmerston; while Curran, Plunkett, O'Connell, and Shiel, were among the brighest ornaments of legal eloquence in modern times. The writings of Swift, Berkeley, Goldsmith, and Moore, can perish but with the use of the English tongue; and in the great drama of military skill and undoubted heroism, surely the Irish Celt has had his share.

What analogy, then, can there be between the Celt and Gladiator, and the African negroes of Virginia? None. The latter are destitute of genius, without glory, non-æsthetic, unprogressive, sensual, stolid, indifferent; not creative, not plastic, not homogeneous. The Caucasian, from the humblest beginning, and with circumstances and opportunity in his favor, will amount to the topmost step in the ladder of fame. Deprived of the tutelage of the white man, every future act of the most civilized negro will be an act of retrogression. The Athenian slaves brought up the rear under Miltiades at the battle of Marathon; and they bore a no less distinguished part in the victory of Platæa.* The Roman slaves, under Tiberius Sempronius Gracchus, beat a Carthaginian army, commanded by Hanno, at

---

* "Ten thousand Lacedæmonian troops held the right wing, *five thousand of whom were Spartans;* and these five thousand were attended by a *body of thirty-five thousand helots,* who were only light-armed—seven to each Spartan."—HERODOTUS.

Beneventum, near Cumæ, during the Campanian war. But the battle of Liberty or Civilization has never yet been fought by the negro race, or by any portion of it. Under the most favorable circumstances, the negro rarely rises in distinction above being the keeper of a second rate saloon or livery stable; nor does he often rank so high even as this. He is ever the servant, but never the ruler of men. One great man, a negro, the world hás yet to see. Whatever may have been his advantages, he has never been able to lift himself up to commonplace, but respectable, mediocrity. Not so the Caucasian, even when contending against the greatest obstacles. Many of the noblest men that ever lived sprang from the humblest grades of life. Demosthenes was the son of a cutler; Epaminondas was born in poverty; the father of Halley was an humble soap boiler; Caius Marius was the child of poor parents; Bunyan was the son of an itinerant tinker; D'Alembert, when an infant, was abandoned by his mother upon the steps of a Catholic Church; Columbus was son to a wool-comber; the sire of De Foe was a butcher; Erasmus was a bastard; and Luther was son to a poor miner. The birth of Shakspeare was humble, indeed; and his advantages of early education extremely limited. Even when he commenced to write his unrivalled plays, he had recourse to the crude Chronicles and Romances of other and indifferent authors, for their superstructure. But whenever the Angel of Creative Genius passed through the grand halls and corridors of his mind, those old books became subject to a new birth—there was then born unto man a rich world of majestic and universal ideas, magically expressed in the purity and harmony of poetic grace—Minerva-like, springing beautiful and immortal from that mind, where the bees of knowledge, love, and wisdom, seem to have deposited their honeyed stores. And the distinction which Shakspeare won in the Dramatic Art, was equally achieved in various departments of the True, the Beautiful, and the Good, by other noble and no less distinguished Caucasians. The same spirit of heavenly interposition which pervades Hamlet, is manifest in the supernal paintings of Raphael also; in the sculpture and architecture of Michel Angelo; in the poetry of Dante; in the Masses of Mozart, and in the Symphonies of Beethoven; in the accumulated wisdom and graceful writings of Göethe; in the deep meditations of Pascal, and the copious eloquence of Bossuet; in the exalted statesmanship of Edmund Burke; in the ineffable grandeur and beauties of Homer; and in the self-sacrificing magnanimity and generous patriotism of Washington.

Now, the loss of any of these Divine men would leave a vacant niche in the philosophy of mind and civilization; while, so far as intellect and its results are concerned, if the whole negro race were obliterated,—if, indeed, the acts of every one of that species of mankind, from the days of Cheops down to the dark reign of Lincoln, were erased or forgotten, Universal History— only in so far as they constitute a link in the perfect order of Nature—would remain the same. Let, then, no Caucasian debase himself by regarding the African negro as his equal. To do so is as great an iniquity, as if he were to seek the exaltation of an equality with angels. His natural place is that in which the Ruler of the heavenly and earthly dominions has placed him from the beginning—at the head of all other branches of our species. Any other affinity than this, would, on his part, be strangely arbitrary and unnatural. For it would be a most difficult effort of the mind, even in an abandoned and confirmed white abolitionist, to imagine a sable Holy Mary or St. Cecilia.

Again, if equal to us in organism and intellectual endowments, it is no less singular than remarkable, that God should have withheld the prophets of His Word from being of their race; since no negro Saviour of Mankind—no Socrates, Isaiah, Brahma, or Mohammed, has yet condescended to enlighten the world with any civilized system of Theogony. Even in the favorite painting of Anti-Slaverydom—Ary Schæfer's "Christus Consolator"—the negro is represented as stretching forth his chained hands for deliverance to that Caucasian Christ, who taught "slaves to obey their masters;" the splendid fiction, of course, belonging to the French poet-painter rather than to the non-æsthetic African. And, until that day when some future negro Solon, Lycurgus, Numa, or Alfred, may impart to his race a code of laws that will reclaim them, and give to them a moral, social, and political *status*, among the nations of the earth—until that race becomes actuated by an exalted principle of self-preservation and advancement, rendering its members plastic and homogeneous— we must certainly be excused for declining a participation of equality and amalgamation with them. Whatever may have been the sins and defects of our own race, its march has been ever forward, and its ambition directed heavenward. Our systems of slavery, even if unjust in the abstract, were often founded upon principles of humanity—always upon the exigencies of nationalities, social, political, and economical necessity—and finally resulted in the partial unification of the various branches of the Caucasian family. And as a combination of the several parts in the machinery of a watch, is necessary to the perfect movement of the whole; so it is that from the commingling of these elements of a common origin and a common destiny, alone, could spring that fine system of international polity, which, in the pride of our vocabulary, we term THE CHRISTIAN CIVILIZATION OF CHRISTENDOM.

XI.

THE great sandy desert, called " Sahara,"—joyless, soundless, lifeless—is not more barren of objects to instruct the naturalist, than is the negro race of incidents interesting to the historian or the philosopher. Having "never invented a reasoned theological system, discovered an alphabet, framed a grammatical language, nor made the least step in science or art"—as Hamilton Smith expresses it—we have to depend upon observation, and the writings of travellers, naturalists, and men of science, for information relative to it. This much, however, is clear, that in ancient Egypt, two thousand years before the birth of Christ, the negro was there as he is here—as he is and has been every where—the servant of a Caucasian master. "Black people"—writes the eminent English Egyptologist, Sir G. Wilkinson—"designated as natives of the foreign land of Cush, are generally represented on the monuments as captives or bearers of tribute to the Pharaohs." This distinguished scholar and antiquary, describes also a painting in a catacomb of Thebes, in which Amunoph III. is represented seated on his throne, receiving the homage and tribute of various nations; among them, the black chiefs of Cush or Ethiopia, with presents of rings of gold, bags of precious stones, "cameleopards, panthers, skins, and long horned cattle, *whose heads are strangely ornamented with the hands and heads of negroes.*" This savage custom, of immolating innumerable victims to turn away the wrath of Deity, or propitiate the anger of a barbarous monarch, as we shall soon see, still prevails in negro-land. As was natural, the contempt of the Egyptians for them was supreme and ineffable. Horus, a King of the nineteenth dynasty, is delineated standing on a platform supported by prostrate negroes; and in a Nubian temple, they are represented as flying in the most abject consternation from the vengeance of Rameses II. But the Egyptian artists were not contented with such displays as these; they chose other symbols to express their contempt for, and the degradation of, the negro. In another Theban painting, he is portrayed in an attitude of servitude, with a salver in his hands; his dress, a scanty apron of the coarsest hide; and the ridiculousness of his *tout ensemble* heightened by the addition of a bob-tail. Nor was it his good fortune to be more highly esteemed by the Arabs. We know from that incomparably enchanting book, "The Thousand-and-one Nights," how the negro was regarded by the Moslems, and that he was their slave. "May Allah disgrace the blacks for their malice and villainy," exclaims Ghânim, the son of Eyoub, upon overhearing Bakheet tell his fellow-negroes, that they would "*roast and eat*" any of the whites who might accidentally fall into their hands. To his inimitable translation, and in particular illustration of this incident, Mr. Lane appended this note: "I am not sure that this is to be understood as a jest; for I have been assured by a slave-dealer and other persons in Cairo, that sometimes slaves brought to that city, *are found to be cannibals;* and that a proof lately occurred there—an infant having been eaten by its black nurse. I was also told that these cannibals are *generally* distinguished by an elongation of the *os coccygis;* or, in other words, that they have tails."

Thus we see that the negro was equally repulsive to the ancient Egyptian and to the modern Arab—that his animality was sternly asserted by each—and that what the Theban painter pictorially represented, is matter of general belief in Cairo. In fact, the opinion that a certain branch of the negro family was adorned by an elongation and outward curvature of the os coccygis has been seriously entertained by some eminent *savans,* and denied by many others, among whom we may name the distinguished Soemmerring. But, be this as it may—and passing the anatomical conformation of the negro over to the consideration of the subject in the succeeding section—the inferior light in which he was regarded by Arab and Egyptian, will be matter neither of wonder nor surprise, to the observer of the African in the Confederate States. Although his social status is here in advance of any that he has ever before occupied in the history of the world, yet his moral and intellectual degradation, dependence, and subordination, are too patent and persistent to admit of doubt. It is not here, however,—where he is comparatively an advanced and civilized being—that we are to search for the genuine characteristics of the typical negro. To properly understand him, he must be regarded as described by enlightened travellers and naturalists; and the opinions of such, we will extract from quotations made by the great English champion of negro equality—Dr. Jas. Cowles Prichard. The negroes of the Gold Coast around the district of Acra, according to this learned author, "are ever on the watch to seize the wives and children of the neighboring clans, and to sell them to strangers: *many sell their own.* Every recess, and every retired corner of the land, has been the scene of hateful rapine and slaughter, not be excused or palliated by the spirit of warfare, but perpetrated in cold blood and for the love of gain." Now, this is the unwilling testimony of a friend *against friends*, whose cause he had undertaken to plead and vindicate; whose descent from Adam and Eve he started out with the predetermined resolution of establishing. Not so the Abbate Bernardo de la Fuente. He was a zealous and pious missionary, wholly devoted to the conversion of the heathen and the preaching of the gospel; but, regardless of consequences, accustomed to speak the truth. Speaking of the Pelagian negroes of the Phillippine Islands, and particularly of the Nigta tribe, he exclaims: "This race of negroes seem to bear upon themselves the malediction of Heaven. They live in the woods and mountains like beasts, in separate families, and wander about supporting themselves by the fruits which the earth spontaneously offers. It has not come to my knowledge that a family of these negroes ever took up their abode in a village. If the Mohammedan inhabitants make slaves of them, they will submit to be beaten to death rather than undergo any bodily fatigue; and it is impossible either by force or persuasion to bring them to labor. Not far from my mission at Buyunan, in the Island de los Negros, there was a horde of negro families who had traffic with some barbarous Indian people, and were by these given to understand that I counselled them to receive baptism, in order that the government might force them to pay tribute: in consequence of this I could never reclaim one of them, and I believe very few negroes have been converted; *for I only found the name of one in a register containing the baptisms of two hundred years.*" This simple and candid statement reflects honor upon the honest sincerity of its author. Had he been one of Exeter Hall's disciples, or still worse, a Yankee missionary, we would have heard annually of the dangers which he had encountered, and of the numerous miraculous conversions that he had wrought; at least the truth would have forever remained hidden from our view. The credulity of the great mass of the American people has long been disgracefully imposed upon in this direction, by the false reports of their religious emissaries abroad. A rational system of theology is intellectually impossible to the negro. Naturally and instinctively he kneels to a Fetiche. Even when, in civilized communities, he adopts a noble and elevated creed, he does so merely as a matter of imitation and formalism; for it is usually beyond the sphere of his reason or metaphysical capacity. But wherever they are placed outside the influence of the surrounding circumstances of civilization, the conversion of negroes is almost an impossibility, and their faith becomes savage and debased. In Western Africa, it is notorious that they worship tigers and other wild animals of prey—trees, beetles, and insects. The best fruit of missionary labor in their midst, according to Father Loyer, is to induce them thus to pray: "My God give me this day rice and yams." They indulge themselves in human sacrifices even at that. M. Seelgrave was an eye-witness, in Old Kalabar, of a child ten months old having been hanged upon a tree with a living fowl, in order to propitiate the deity and cause a sick king to recover his health. And it may not have escaped the memory of the reader, that the King of Dahomeh sacrificed to *his* god, out of gratitude for one of his victories, four thousand Fidans, causing their heads to be cut off and piled up together in a pyramidal heap. When this miserable savage died, the same tragedy was reënacted, but upon a still more terrible and gigantic scale.

No less cruel or barbarous are the details of a Cannibal Festival, as detailed in a letter of Rev. Peter W. Bernaske, dated Whydah, (Abomey), November 29th, 1860. "On the eve of the day," says he, "when the custom was to commence, the whole town slept at King's gate, and got up at 5 o'clock in the morning to weep. And so they hypocritically did. The lamentations did not continue more than ten minutes; and before the King came out to fire guns to give notice to all, more than one hundred souls had been sacrificed, besides the same number of women killed in the inside of the palace. Ninety chief captains, one hundred and twenty princes and princesses—all these carried out separately, human beings, by four and two, to sacrifice for the late King." On the 1st of August—a few days after this event—the dusky monarch, with a funeral cortege, came out to bury the remains of his father, with the following living things—"Sixty men, fifty rams, fifty goats, forty cocks, drakes, cowries, &c. The men and women soldiers, well armed with muskets and blunderbusses for firing; and when he was gone round his palace, he came to the gate and fired plenty; and there he killed fifty of the poor creatures and saved ten." Fifteen days after this, the missionary was summoned before his majesty, when he beheld upon the palace gate "ninety human heads cut off that morning, their blood flowing on the ground like a flood, and the heads carefully laid on swish beds for public view." Three days afterward, he saw "at the same gate, sixty heads laid upon the same place; and on three days again, thirty-six fresh heads in the same position." The king had four platforms erected in the market place, from which "he threw cowries and cloths to the people, and then sacrificed about sixty souls." "I dare say," continues the missionary, that "he killed more than two thousand; because he kills men outside to be seen by all, and women inside privately. Oh! he destroyed many souls during this wicked custom." Such being the normal religion of the negro, who will wonder that the rational theism of the Abbate Fuente and his predecessors, should have fallen as vainly upon his ears, as the harvest seed doth upon barren rocks?

The Hottentot or Bosjesman tribe—the negro "Bushmen" of South Africa—are described by M. Bory de St. Vincent as forming the transition between man and the genera of Orangs and Gibbons. "These people," he adds, "are so brutish, lazy, and stupid, that the idea of reducing them to slavery has been abandoned." To this, the most profound advocate of the "unity of race" theory is constrained to add his testimony. "Without houses or even huts," writes Dr. Prichard, "living in caves and holes in the earth, those naked and half-starved savages wander through forests, in small companies or separate families, hardly supporting their comfortless existence by collecting wild roots; by a toilsome search for the eggs of ants; and by devouring, whenever they can catch them, lizards, snakes, and the most loathsome insects." Surely, if consistent and sincere, the self-abasement of this gentleman would border on the sublime; but when we remember that in the fullness of his English pride, he would hardly admit that the Irish Celt was a child of Eve, the fraternal humiliation with which he embraces the degraded Hottentot, and claims for him common origin with himself, is stripped of more than half its poetic *fancy*. Yet, in matters of veracity, the distance that divides Dr. Prichard from the recent, and somewhat celebrated traveller, Dr. David Livingstone, is painfully astonishing. Sydney Smith it was, we believe, who declared it would take a surgical operation to drive a joke into a Scotchman; and certainly it would require some similar experiment to force the truth out of this *Scotch* missionary. Does he know of aught debasing or hopeless in the negro character? Having, perhaps, the fear of Exeter Hall before his eyes, it is carefully concealed. If he cannot speak glowingly of his African friends, he will be sufficiently cautious not to speak evil of them. Relative to the manners, customs and characteristics of the Hottentots, he simply informs us that their " hair " " springs from the scalp in tufts with bare spaces between;" while of the black natives of Basongo, he says, that he was impressed by the strong " resemblance they bore to certain notabilities at home !" There is one tribe, however, in speaking descriptively of which he never seems to weary—the Batoka. " They have," he says, " a curious taste for ornamenting their villages with the skulls of strangers." " They follow," he adds, " the curious custom of knocking out the front teeth at the age of puberty. This is done by both sexes; and though the under teeth, being relieved from the attrition of the upper, grow long and somewhat bent out, and thereby cause the under lip to protrude in a most unsightly way, no young woman thinks herself accomplished until she has got rid of the upper incisors. This custom gives them an uncouth, old-like appearance. Their laugh is hideous." And again : "The women clothe themselves better than the Balonda, but the men go '*in puris naturalibus.*' They walk about without the smallest sense of shame. They have even lost the tradition of the 'fig leaf.' I asked a fine, large-bodied old man if he did not think it would be better to adopt a little covering. He looked with a pitying leer, and laughed with surprise at my thinking him at all indecent; he evidently considered himself above such weak superstition. * * * It was considered a good joke when I told them that, if they had nothing else, they must put on a bunch of grass." In conclusion : "their mode of salutation is quite singular. They throw themselves on the ground, and, rolling from side to side, slap the outside of their thighs as expressions of thankfulness and welcome, uttering the words 'kina bomba.'" That we have so much of the truth from Dr. Livingstone, even in so mild and amiable a form, is doubtless due to the facts, that a portion of the Batoka rebelled against his authority, and that a war of extermination was waged against them by his pet negro chieftain, one Sebituane, whose personal narratives are absolutely compared by him to Cæsar's Commentaries !

But to turn to another far different and more reliable source.—M. Lesson, in speaking of the Alforas— a tribe of New Guinea negroes—states that "the custom prevalent among them of putting their pris-

oners to death and erecting their spoils as trophies,
accounts for the difficulty found in observing" their
habits and customs even upon their own soil. "But,"
he continues, "the Papuas described them to us as of a
ferocious character—cruel and gloomy; possessing no
arts, and passing their whole lives in seeking subsistence
in the forests. * * * An excessive stupidity was
stamped upon their countenances. These savages, whose
skin is of a very deep, swarthy, dirty brown or dark
color, go naked. They make incisions upon their arms
and breasts, and wear in their noses pieces of wood
nearly six inches long. Their character is taciturn, and
their physiognomy fierce; their motion is uncertain and
slow." To the foregoing the enterprising and accomplished Dr. Leyden adds his testimony. It is to him
that the world is indebted for the first elaborate and
intelligent account of the Alforas. "They are," says
he, "universally rude and unlettered; *and where they
have not been reduced to the state of slaves of the soil,*
their habits have a general resemblance. The most
singular feature of their manners is the necessity imposed on each and all of them, at some period of life, to
imbrue their hands in human blood; and in general,
among all their tribes, as well as the Idan, no person is
permitted to marry till he can show the skull of a man
whom he has slaughtered. They eat the flesh of their
enemies, like the Battas, and drink out of their skulls;
and the ornaments of their houses are human skulls and
teeth, which are consequently in great request among
them." In describing the negroes of Maria and Van
Dieman's Islands, Mr. Heron says of them, that "they
are without laws or anything like regular government;
without arts of any kind, with no idea of agriculture, of

the use of metals, or of the services to be derived from
animals; without clothes or fixed abode, and with no
other shelter than a mere shed of bark to keep off the
cold south winds; and with no arms but a club and
spear. Although these and the neighboring New Hol-
landers are placed in a fine climate and productive soil,
they derive no other sustenance from the earth than a
few fern roots and bulbs of orchises; and they are often
driven by the failure of their principal resource, fish, to
the most revolting food—frogs, lizards, serpents, spiders,
the larvæ of insects, and particularly a kind of large
caterpillar, found in groups on the branches of the
eucalyptus resinifera. They are sometimes obliged to
appease the cravings of hunger by the bark of trees and
by a paste made by pounding together ants, their larvæ,
and fern roots. Their remorseless cruelty, their unfeel-
ing barbarity to women and children, their immoderate
revenge for the most trivial affronts, their want of
natural affection, *are hardly redeemed by the slightest
traits of goodness.* When we add that they are quite
insensible to distinctions of right and wrong, destitute of
religion, without any idea of a Supreme Being, and with
the feeblest notion, if there be any at all, of a future
state, the revolting picture is complete in all its features." It would be easy, if necessary, to swell this
dreary record; but we have already gone over sufficient
ground—we have seen the typical negro in at least
one-half the latitudes and longitudes of his native
home—everywhere we have found him hopelessly lazy,
filthy, savage, and degraded unto beastliness. And thus
have they lived and perished for untold centuries, Christ-
less and Godless, starving in their huts and kraals,
burrowing like rabbits into the earth for shelter, roam-

ing through forests and over mountain sides stark naked, living upon polluted things that even birds and beasts of prey, would scorn to touch, and, finally, sinking into earth like decayed vegetable matter—without a name— without a history—without a monument to record that they had ever lived or died. And all their past but symbolizes what shall be their eternal future, unless brought under 'the complete and unconditional direction and control of the Caucasian race. In this condition of subordination and dependence, the whole negro family might in time become' what the four or five millions of them now in the Confederate States of America are—useful, affectionate, well cared for, happy and contented, and semi-civilized servants. But to the distinction of being a self-ruling and self-sustaining people, they never have risen, and never can arise; for their own inherent organism prohibits it. Their normal state is that of servitude and subjection; and their characteristics even when so placed, we will leave the eminent scholar from whom we have already quoted, at the commencement of this section, to relate: "The negro mind [when domesticated] is confiding and single-hearted, naturally kind and hospitable. *Both sexes are easily ruled, and appreciate what is good under the guidance of common justice and prudence.* Yet where so much that honors human nature remains in apathy—the typical woolly-haired races have never invented a reasoned theological system, discovered an alphabet, framed a grammatical language, nor made the least step in science or art. *They have never comprehended what they have learned, or retained a civilization taught them by contact with more refined nations,* as soon as *that contact ceased.* They have at no time formed great political

States, nor commenced a self-evolving civilization. Conquest with them has been confined to kindred tribes, and produced only slaughter. Even Christianity of more than three centuries' duration in Congo has scarcely excited a progressive civilization.". And thus are we fortified in our position, by the opinion of one of the most candid and learned of English naturalists— that it is from the so-called institution of "Slavery," and only from this, can spring the regeneration of the negro race.

XII.

How comes it, then, that the negro is, and ever has been, normally savage? He was, from the first, surrounded by the earliest civilization. He came in contact with the greatest people of antiquity. He witnessed the sun of enlightenment and progress irradiating the world around him, as early at least as four thousand years ago; yet he remained, throughout the long ages, stolid, immovable, indifferent, unchangeable, and revolting to the geniality of all superior races, as the burning mountains and sandy deserts of his native land. Memphis and Thebes, Babylon and Nineveh, arose in splendor and magnificence; the pyramids of Egypt and Ethiopia were built for immortality; the Phœnicians were spreading letters and commerce, the Greeks and Romans, liberty and civilization: but upon the remaining monuments of all, the negro is displayed in a condition of abject subjugation, degradation, and slavery; while in no part of all Africa has there been discovered an alphabet, a hieroglyphic, a picture, or a symbol, as the remains of his intelligence or ingenuity. We shall

4

endeavor to account for all this. We will undertake to
prove that the negro family constitute a distinct and
entirely different group of the human species from the
Caucasian—that their physical and intellectual organization is radically dissimilar and inferior to that of the
white man—and consequently that servitude and subordination, under the supervision of the wiser and governing races, is their natural and unalterable relation in
life. In seeking to establish this, we shall hardly
hazard an opinion of our own, not substantiated by the
experimental demonstrations of the most illustrious
anatomists and *savants* that have ever lived. We do
not believe, with M. de St. Vincent, that the negro
constitutes the connecting link between man and the
Simiæ. That position in natural history more properly
belongs to the Gorilla. Of this creature, in a work
recently published by him, M. Duchaillu concludes that
there is a dissimilarity between the bony frame of man
and that of the gorilla, but that there is also "*an awful
likeness,* which in the gorilla resembles an exaggerated
caricature of a human being." The first specimen of
this genus seen by him, he describes as " some hellish
dream creature—a being of that hideous order, half-
man, half-beast, which is found pictured by old artists
in representations of the infernal regions." Upon
being shot, he adds, the gorilla uttered " a groan which
*had something terribly human in it, and yet was full of
brutishness.*" The negro proper is certainly not so low
in the scale of *physical** organism as the gorilla; yet

---

* In another portion of his work, Du Chaillu gives a frightful
account of the cannibalism prevailing among certain negro tribes;
particularly the Fans, from which we make a few brief extracts:

it is demonstrable that he (especially the Hottentot), most certainly approximates in the structure of his frame to the monkey kind and the troglodyte. Their women, particularly those of the Bosjesman, according to Soemmerring, Sonneret, and Barrow, are marked by an elongation of the nymphæ, which increases with age and maturity, and often reaches to the startling length of five or seven inches; but this, however, is not a charac-

---

"On going out one morning, I saw a pile of ribs, leg and arm-bones, and skulls (human) piled up at the back of my house, which looked horrid enough to me. In fact, symptoms of cannibalism *stare me in the face wherever I go.* Eating the bodies of persons who have died of sickness, is a form of cannibalism of which I had never heard among any people, so that I determined to inquire if it were indeed a general custom among the Fans, or merely an exceptional freak. They spoke without embarrassment about the whole matter, and I was informed that they constantly buy the dead of the Osheba tribe, who, in return, buy theirs. They also buy the dead of other families in their own tribes; and besides this, get the bodies of a great many slaves from the Mbichos and Mbondemos, for which they readily give ivory, at the rate of a small tusk for a body. * * * A party of Fans, who came down on the sea-shore, once actually stole a freshly buried body from the cemetery, cooked it and ate it; * * and even the missionaries heard of it, for it happened at a village not far from the missionary grounds. * * * In fact, the Fans seem regular ghouls, only they practice their horrid custom unblushingly, and in open day, and have no shame about it. I have seen here knives covered with human skin, which their owners valued very highly. To-day, the Queen brought me some boiled plantain, which looked very nice; but the fear lest she should have cooked it in some pot where a man had been cooked before—which was most likely the case—made me unable to eat it. On these journeys, I have fortunately taken with me sufficient pots to do my own cooking. They are the *finest, bravest looking set of negroes I have seen in the interior,* and eating human flesh seems to agree with them." Certainly the *morals* of the Fans cannot be far in advance of those of the gorilla.

teristic of the simiæ. They have also, generally after their first pregnancy, a most ridiculous and disgusting protuberance on their buttocks, which is exaggerated in aspect by the remarkable outward extension of the posterior, and inward curvature of the spine; and this latter, it may be observed here, is a distinctive peculiarity in the structure of the race. The projection in question, it is said, ordinarily reaches five or six inches in length from the apex of the spine, and imparts to the women when walking the most ludicrous appearance imaginable—"every step being accompanied with a quivering and tremulous motion, as if two masses of jelly were attached behind." This was one of the distinguishing features discovered by Baron Cuvier in the "Hottentot Venus," exhibited some years ago in Paris—a Venus which certainly must have been a very Hottentotish Venus. We can easily comprehend why extreme loveliness, was the cause of all Mary, Queen of Scots' misfortunes, and why those heavenly attributes, in spite of her faults and follies, and three centuries of time, still endear her memory to millions of men; but we are unable to conceive by what miracle, or divine interposition, a chivalrous sympathy could be aroused in a refined and generous mind, on behalf of a Hottentot venus or queen. Yet it is not because that the latter is wanting in charms of personal beauty that we would deem her an inferior being, but because that Nature has made her with a hopelessly degraded intellectual organization.

Dr. Soemmerring enumerates forty-six instances wherein the anatomy of the negro differs from that of the Caucasian. In his summary of the characteristics of the negro *cranium*, Mr. Lawrence describes the

whole front of the head as narrow, the forehead flattened and receding; the cavity of the brain comparatively small, both in its circumference and full length
measurements; the hinder perforation and condyles
placed farther back than in the European; the face
large, jaws prominent, teeth slanting, chin receding,
and cheek-bone extraordinarily arched and projecting
forward; the nasal cavity small, and the *ossa nasa*
nearly consolidated—the whole structure, in these and
many other particulars, he says, "unequivocally approximating to that of the monkey. Compared with
the Caucasian, the intellectual qualities are reduced
and the animal features enlarged. And this inferiority
of organization is attended with the corresponding unfailing inferiority of faculties." A very clever writer
on this subject, has ascertained that the brain of the
white man averages ninety-two to ninety-five cubic
inches, while that of the negro often falls as low as
seventy-five inches, and rarely exceeds eighty; and, as
we have seen above, its locality as greatly inclines to
the posterior of the head, as it does to the anterior in
that of the Caucasian. Hence, it must be self-evident
to the most superficial thinker, that a negro of well
regulated intellectual faculties, such as any ordinary
white man possesses, is absolutely a natural impossibility. Even his vocal and lingual inferiority is sternly
marked and decisive. No negro ever spoke a civilized
tongue correctly, much less, perfectly. It is an indisputable fact, that the French language learned of
French masters by the negroes in Hayti, is rapidly
becoming corrupted or falling into disuse, and the
mother African dialect instinctively taking its place—
another patent illustration of their incapacity to retain

a borrowed civilization, without the controlling supervision of a superior race. The musical faculties of the
negro are equally defective. No great composer—no
great singer even—of this family, we believe, has ever
existed. The famous "Black Swan," *who was of a
mixed type*, and who was reputed by the friends and
admirers of the African as a musical prodigy, constitutes no exception to this inevitable rule. In the fullness of England's philanthropy, she was parentally
placed under the care and tutorship of the British
Queen's musician; but notwithstanding the most strenu-
ous efforts on her behalf, the sacred charge had to be
relinquished, and the "Swan" proved a miserable
failure. The negro, it is true, fancies music; so he
does the most gaudy and glaring colors. This fancy,
however, is sensual, not intellectual. The solemn elephant and the gallant war-steed, are equally moved by
the influence of harmony. But the emotions kindled in
the bosoms of a Scottish regiment, by the air of "Annie
Laurie," and which could drive their bayonets through
the serried columns of a Russian army at Inkerman, are
intellectual emotions—memories of mountain homes,
childhood's scenes, absent friends, and therefore, stimu-
lating to glory and immortality—but as impossible to
the subjectiveness of the typical negro, as they would
be to the elephant or the war-horse.

It is not in the locality of mind alone that the negro
is an inferior being; debasement characterizes, in indel-
ible particulars, his whole skeleton. His head, even
superficially considered, will convey to the ordinary
observer this conviction. It is prognathous, and, therefore, of a type with simiæ. Soemmerring found that
the position of the *foramen magnum*, in the skull of

the negro, approximated to its situation in that of the Chimpanzee and Ourang-Outang. This famous anatomist also discovered, among many other similar peculiarities—and his conclusions in this particular are acquiesced in by the no less distinguished Daubenton,—that the head of the negro is placed farther back upon the column (vertebral) of the spine, than is the case with any of the superior races; which is another distinguishing feature of animal construction. The bones of his leg are bent outward. The outer and smaller bone (fibula), and the larger of the bones (tibia) forming the segment of the leg, are, in the negro, convex. The calves of his legs are so high as to encroach upon his hams. His feet and hands, instead of being arched as with the Caucasian, are flat. The os calcis with him is almost in a direct straight line. As is the case with the ape and troglodyte, his forearm is proportionally much longer than that of the European. But the distinction does not stop here. Dr. Vrolik, in making a comparative examination of the conformation of the pelvis in various races, was enabled to arrive at some discoveries and conclusions at once important and interesting to us. "The pelvis of the male negro," he avers, "in the strength and density of its substance, and of the bones which compose it, resembles the pelvis of a wild beast." The pelvis of the negress, however, he found to be of lighter substance and greater delicacy both of form and structure, but still so gross as to render it impossible to separate it from the idea of degradation in type, if not immediate approximation to the form of that in the lower animals. The pelvis of the Hottentot, especially, forcibly resembled the structure of that in simiæ.

We will now direct our attention to the apparent

characteristics which distinguish this genus of man, and adopt the definition which the most illustrious naturalist that ever lived, gives of the negro proper. " The negro race," says Cuvier, "is marked by a black' complexion, crisped or woolly hair, compressed cranium, and a flat nose. The projection of the lower parts of the face, and the thick lips, evidently approximate it to the monkey tribe. The hordes of which it consists have always remained in the most complete state of barbarism," &c., &c. Malpighi was the first anatomist who discovered a membrane, or layer, beneath the cuticle, which he asserted was the seat of the black color in the negro's skin. More recently, however, M. Flourens, a justly celebrated French anatomist, made a more thorough and minute examination of this phenomenon, which enabled him to arrive systematically at a most important discovery. Between the cutis (skin) and cuticle (scarf-skin) of the negro, he found *four* layers; the *second* of which, from the cutis, had the aspect of a mucous membrane, and upon the surface of which was spread *a layer of black pigment.* This membrane is entirely foreign to the organism of the white man. M. Flourens had this *pigmentum nigrum* denuded by maceration, when it appeared of a much blacker hue than it had previously presented. He had this experiment subsequently displayed before the Academy of Sciences, in Paris, by macerating the skins both of a typical negro and mulatto, each of whom were possessed of this phenomenon; but upon subjecting the white man to a similar process of examination, it was found that the pigment, and the membrane upon which it is deposited in the negro, were completely wanting in his structure. When the results of M. Flourens' discoveries were published, Dr. Henle—a very clever German anatomist—received them with unfeigned scepticism, and, resolved upon testing their reliability, subjected the pigment to a microscopical examination. The results of his minute labor, however, only enabled him to arrive in effect at similar conclusions. But what M. Flourens regarded as a membrane, Dr. Henle maintains is composed of complicated cells or cytoblasts. But, *in addition* to those cells which characterize the organization of the Caucasian, he frankly confesses to having discovered *other and different* cells in the structure of the negro, which are the seat of the black pigment, and necessarily of his outward deformed aspect.

Here, then, is a phenomenon, distinct, and peculiar to the structure of the African race, and bearing the signal stamp of degradation and inferiority of type. If, as their white advocates claim for them, they are equally with the Caucasian, children of Adam and Eve, how have they become possessed of separate characteristics in their anatomical organization, and which are so entirely foreign to our structure? If *we* ever were possessed of them, when did our race lose them? If, in the beginning, *they* had them not, then when, where, and how, did *they* become the sole possessors of these exclusive traits? It will not do to argue that the moles, freckles, and similar phenomena of the white races, must also have some peculiar seat of color; for these are evanescent and abnormal, while the black pigment and the *additional* membrane in the negro, are normal, enduring, and unalterable, as the eternity of granite hills!

Relative to the color, crispness, and woolly aspect of the negro's hair, men of learning and science in the

Old World, where the opportunities of observation are comparatively limited, have long varied in opinion as to the cause. It is now, however, a fact well established in this country, that the several peculiar characteristics of this excrescence, are, in the same manner as the coloration in the negro's skin, influenced by organic and exclusive agencies. Peter A. Browne, Esq., of Philadelphia, in his complete refutation of the conclusion arrived at by Dr. Prichard—that the negro has hair, properly so called, and not wool—gives us the results of his very thorough and scientific investigations. He subjected the pile (hair) of three different types of mankind to a microscopical examination—Indian, Caucasian, and Negro. By this process, he distinctly discovered that the hair of the native American Indian was cylindrical; that of the Caucasian oval; and that of the Negro eccentrically elliptical. "In observing the *course* or *path* pursued by the point where it pierces the epidermis (bark of the skin) to its apex," he found that the pile of each had respectively its own specific and individual variety of type. That of the Indian was lank and straight—of the Caucasian, flowing, wavy, or curled—and of the Negro, crisped, frizzled, spiral, and woolly. The *quality* of each of these specific species of pile, is dependent for its particular *form* upon certain constitutional elementary causes. The necessary physiology of a cylindrical hair is lankness and straightness; that of the oval renders it imperative that it shall wave, or curl, or flow, in its course; but the eccentrically elliptical hair, in obedience to the law of its nature, is crisped, spiral, or woolly. In exposing these several forms of pile, to a chemical and mechanical experiment under the microscope, for the purpose of testing the relative properties of ductility and elasticity of their fibres, it was found that these forces in the cylindrical hair were *equal* on all sides, and, therefore, naturally straight and lank; whereas, in the oval hair, the shrinking and stretching powers proved *unequal*—the fibres on the two flattened sides of the filament being more powerful than those on the ellipsoid, and, consequently, of a curving tendency in its path. But when thus tested, the pile of the negro still retained, in the same manner, its spiral and woolly characteristic.

The *inclination* of pile is entirely due "to the angle which the root of the hair bears to the skin of the animal in which it is imbedded. The roots both of cylindrical and oval pile have an oblique angle of inclination, for which reason those hairs do not grow out of the epidermis at a right angle thereto, but inclined in a determinate manner; while the roots of wool, which is eccentrically elliptical or flat, on the contrary, lie in the dermis *perpendicularly*, and hence the filaments pierce the epidermis at *right angles* thereto." Now, this latter prominent and specific difference is, among all mankind, the peculiarly exclusive characteristic of the negro race. Some tribes of Papuas, inhabiting the north coast of Guinea, called "Mopheads," are said by Dr. Prichard to have "a bushy mass of *half*-woolly hair," but it is now notorious that these are a bastard genus, begotten of an amalgamation of Malays and negroes.

All pile is furnished by nature with a particular seat of color. We have seen above that the characteristic of the Caucasian's skin is discoloration, whereas the negro is furnished with an *additional* membrane, or cellular substances, totally foreign to the organism of the former, but which is the instrument of coloration in the

latter. The same diversity, but in another aspect, presents itself in the physiology of pile. In addition to its
cortex (cover) and intermediate fibres, the hair of the
white man has a complicated and delicately constructed
canal, through which this coloring matter flows; and
where color even fails, the canal remains, but void of
the coloring substance. The wool of the negro, however, has no such canal. The coloring matter here,
when present, permeates the cortex and its intermediate
fibres—forming part and parcel of the filament. Thus,
in the skin of the Caucasian we find *no* organ of coloration, but in that of the negro we find a *specific membrane* for that purpose. On the contrary, the hair of
the white man *is* furnished with a canal, which is the
medium of its coloring qualities; of this machinery,
however, the wool of the negro is altogether devoid.
Consequently, "the hair of the white man is perfect,
having not only the apparatus found in other pile, but
one exclusively belonging to itself—a central canal for
the conveyance of coloring matter;" it is oval in shape,
in its direction curling or flowing, and *acutely* angled
out of the epidermis, from which it springs. The wool
of the negro is the direct opposite, being an imperfect
pile, having no central canal, flat in shape, and issuing
out of the dermis, through the surface of the epidermis,
in right angle. When this pile is subjected to a microscopical examination, its surface, or angles, present ser-
rations such as are found upon the wool of sheep. These
scales in the Caucasian are *rudimentary*, but on the hair
of the negro, they are *perfect*. On the pile of the
former, they are comparatively few in number and of
smooth surface, rounded points, and closely embracing
the shaft. On the hair of the negro, they are promi-

nent, numerous, and transparent; and this species of pile *will felt*, while that of the white man will *not*. Hence, the conclusions arrived at are: that hair and wool are not the same integuments; that hair, properly so called, is cylindrical or oval in shape, and wool eccentrically elliptical or flat; that the direction of the former is straight, flowing, or curling, but that of the latter crisped, or spirally frizzled; that hair issues out of the epidermis at an acute angle, while wool emerges out of the dermis at a right angle; that the coloring matter of hair is provided with a central canal, and that of wool disseminated throughout the cortex and its intermediate fibres; that the scales on hair are comparatively few in number, smooth, less pointed, and more closely embracing the shaft, while in wool they are numerous, rough, pointed, and do not intimately embrace the shaft; that hair will not felt, but wool will; finally, that the covering of the negro's head will felt and is wool; and, therefore, that he is of a different type of mankind from the latter, and by no means children of *one* common progenitor.

We have now demonstrated that the negro is an inferior being—that he is not of the same origin, organism, moral or intellectual faculties as the white man—and that to insist, in defiance of historic and scientific evidences, that he is descended from the same parents that we are, is the most false and insulting blasphemy against Nature and truth. Neither can the matter be mended by amalgamation.* Nature ever indignantly rejects or

---

* All animated nature scorns amalgamation. The beasts of the forest—the birds of the air—the fishes of the sea—all keep, as a general rule, their own tribes, or species, free from this sin against

revenges, all artificial interferences with the wisdom, unity, and harmony of her immutable laws.   The Spaniards, who settled in Mexico and Central America, were noble Caucasians—were the descendants of the Cid, Ponce de Leon, and Bernardo del Carpio—descendants of the conquerors of Granada and the victors of Lepanto—children of those daring or chivalrous adventurers, who wrested from Montezuma his fair dominions and golden palaces, and sought to explore the Mississippi and Missouri to their sources—yet where, and what, are their Mexican progeny of to-day?   They married and intermarried with the natives; amalgamation was gradually followed by decay and emasculation; and for the noble Pelasgic countenances of the loyal subjects of Isabel the Catholic, we seek in vain among the half-Aztec, half-monkey physiognomies of those regions.   On the other hand, the Ethiopians, who, in some superficial aspects, *seem* to approximate to the negro, have for thousands of years—certainly long before the flight into Egypt—chosen a great portion of the women for their harems, from among the slave women of the Soudan, without becoming negroes themselves, or having their race even perceptibly corrupted.   And, again, we know from the very satisfactory work of Dr. Van Evrie— "Negroes and Negro Slavery"—that hybridity in the American States is invariably attended with a corresponding diminution of virility, from the first generation of mulattoism to the fourth, when it becomes "as absolutely sterile as muleism:" all of which facts demonstrate, that the Utopian dreams of misguided and per-

---

the great *kosmos* of a superintending Providence, unless thwarted by the ingenious and artificial contrivances and experiments of man.

verse modern philanthropy, on behalf of the negro, are impossible of realization; and that the proper social and political sphere of the latter is subserviency to the superior genius of the Caucasian.

NOTE.—Well meaning and excellent minds may accuse the author of infidelity to the Mosaic account of creation, because of the doctrines promulged by him in the foregoing section of his essay. To all such persons—if there be any—he responds: "If other men choose to misinterpret Moses, it is neither his fault nor the fault of Moses."

We contend that the genus, man, like unto all of the other types of animated nature, was created in distinctive and specific groups, during certain *intervals* of creation; like the buffalo, Durham, and Kerry cow—like the salmon, trout, and rockfish—like the jay, mocking, and canary birds. But here we run counter again to the popular notions of the Biblical account. The "days" of Genesis are made to represent such days as we recognize. God, of course, might as easily have created the world in the twinkling of an eye, if such were his purpose, as in the "six days" of our ordinary theology, or, indeed, in a billion of *our* years. But the work of creation—of decomposition and formation—is still going on; and the usual interpretation given to the words of Moses, place him and the science of Nature at eternal enmity, where nought but harmony should exist. The Hebrew word *ioum*, which represents the "morning and evening" of the successive *cycles* of Creation, in the book of Genesis, has been restricted in the accepted English translation to the term "day." *Ioum*, however, may mean either "day" or any unlimited period of time. Hence, in the Commentaries of St. Augustine, that great light of the Latin church, we find that he is not far from adopting the broader signification of the term; whilst Nemesius, a Greek bishop of the fourth century, did not hesitate to regard *ioum* as synonymous with the Syriac word *sar*, or cycle of revolution.

Let Moses and the prophets, for the future, be judged by the lights of nature, science, and philosophy. They have suffered too long from the stupid interpretations of dogmatism and scepticism—twin-sisters, like sin and death, who have done more than all other powers to breed INFIDELITY.

XIII.

THE philosophy of Don Quixote was the insanity of misdirected Chivalry. In like manner, the pilgrims of Plymouth Rock are actuated by a wicked and perverse system of unnatural philanthropy. The woeful-faced Knight of La Mancha, went forth into the world to overthrow sorcery, magic, and the general machinery of darkness—he would make all things right, redress wrong, and liberate helpless and innocent maidens from the thraldom of the devil—but, alas! his giants were inoffensive wind-mills, his opposing armies harmless sheepfolds. But the master of Sancho was sincere—was the creature and victim of his own illusions—was innocent and guileless toward the human family. The pilgrim zealots of New England, with "humanity" and "philanthropy" upon their lips, and jealousy and hatred of the Southern labor system stamped upon their hearts, make war upon the constitutional rights of fifteen free, sovereign, and independent States, to gratify their malice and glorify their immaculateness (hypocrisy), *at the expense of others*—invariably in the name, and professedly on the behalf, but always to the irreparable injury and disadvantage of, the negro race—until they have at length succeeded, by means of this shibboleth, in destroying the greatest Republic upon earth, and arraying against each other, in a bloody civil war, thirty millions of freemen! The psychology of these men is sheer dissimulation—historical and almost transparent. They are nothing, if they are not pragmatical. Those who kneel not before the same altar with them, are not only proscribed in this life, but consigned to future perdition in the next. He who would dare to differ from them in political opinion, must learn how to resign himself to contumely and obscurity. Every six or seven years, they will become possessed of some new spirit of reform, to the teachings of which their neighbors must bend, or reap the dire consequences of their recusancy. Their Puritan ancestors of England were the same. They had their lawful king sent to the block. They placed the reins of power in the hands of a vulgar usurper, murderer, blasphemer, and tyrant. They banished from the throne the line of kings, to whom, by inheritance, it legally belonged, and they placed upon it, men who were as far removed from being gentlemen, as the Puritans were from being saints. When their enormities became unendurable at home, they wandered over to Holland, where they were sheltered with a temporary asylum. But their hypocrisy, studied eccentricities, long lank hair, rueful countenances, snivelling cant, affectations of supernatural self-gloriousness, and revolting habits of impertinent officiousness, soon rendered them at once obnoxious and intolerable there.

They next emigrated to, and settled in, Massachusetts. Here, in the virgin forests of a new land, they planted the banner of intolerance, and erected altars and temples to the deity of human sacrifice. They had Roman Catholics sent to the gibbet; they butchered Quakers in cold blood; they caused old women, charged with witch-

5

craft by vagrants and prostitutes, to perish at the stake; and they banished, like lepers from their midst, Baptists and Methodists. Nor have their progeny, down to the present day, improved, save in proportion as the outside influences of social forces compelled them. But a few years since, they laid in ashes the charitable institutions and religious edifices of the Roman Catholics; and in violation of the Federal Constitution, they sought to exclude members of this denomination, and especially foreigners, from citizenship. They next sought to regulate the appetites of society, and directly violate the Constitution, by the provisions of the famous "Maine Law," which prohibited the sale or importation of spirituous liquors. Now they are devoted followers of the notorious Fanny Wright, and bent upon the fundamental overthrow of the Christian institution of matrimony. Next we find them propagandists of the philosophy of Charles Fourier, and determinedly resolved upon the subversion of the rights of personal property and the establishment of Communism.

But during the past twenty-five or thirty years, the very spine of all northern and puritanical fanaticism, has been ANTI-SLAVERY. Circumstances, and the contiguity of the sea, nevertheless, had rendered the people of New England navigators. As such, they were among the first on this continent to eagerly engage in, and profit by the slave trade, and certainly the last to relinquish it. When our government resolved upon its abolition, many of their representatives opposed the measure in Congress to the bitter end. Having been previously slave traders, and the influx of immigrants, as well as an uncongenial climate, rendering slave labor unprofitable, they gradually commenced the abolition of slavery, amongst themselves, and forthwith began a systematic assault upon the institutions of the States which retained it. By stealth and loud professions of self-righteousness, their aggressions increased ; until at length they had the country divided by an unconstitutional line of demarkation, indicating *their* portion of the land as supremely Christian, and the *other* as eminently pagan. Notwithstanding that they themselves had bought, or kidnapped from Africa, and sold as merchandise, the very negroes, or their ancestors, over whom they now shed crocodile tears, they resolved upon annoying those who were the possessors and owners of them, and in due time to rob them of their property. Thus they commenced that unchristian agitation, whereby the peace of our country was distracted, and the happiness of the negro diminished. Sworn to protect and uphold the Federal Compact; and the Constitution having specially provided for the protection of slave property—northern legislators soon converted official perjury into a morality, and organized themselves into a political league of professional negro stealers. Having, by Satanic promises and fair words, charmed away many of those docile and credulous creatures, they abandoned them to their own unfortunate fate, or shipped them naked, hungry and helpless, to the frigid climates of Canada or Newfoundland. Even those of them who remain in the abolition States, are deprived of all, or nearly all, natural, *social*, and political rights. In most of these States the negro is debarred from the exercise of the elective franchise. In others, before he can vote, he must have a specified property qualification. In the great commercial emporium of the late Union, New York, he is not permitted to ride in a public omnibus. He can be accommodated

in the city railroad cars, only in those which are designated on the outside as being privileged to him; and
these even are limited to a few lines.   Indeed, amongst
the abolitionists generally, the negro is degraded, a
vagabond and an outcast—the butt of humor and ribald
jest—a machine for crime, or for the villain and black-
leg's dirty work—and always used as the medium of
self-laudation by the hypocrite; as the temple was by
the Pharisee.   He is seldom employed by the white
man—never when it can be avoided, unless as a barber,
a cartman, or a table-waiter.   He is not associated with,
but by persons of his own class and color.   As a general
rule, he is neither a lawyer nor an editor; never the
white man's parson.   Even the pews of the Christian
churches, excepting those of the Roman Catholic denomination, are closed against him.   The people do not
understand him—do not care for him—feel that they
have no special interest in him—have no sympathy,
that is not purely objective, with him—and treat him
only as a medium of "moral" excitement, precisely as
they have used for fashionable purposes, the opera,
Maria Monk, Heenan, the carcass of Bill Poole, Barnum, and Louis Kossuth.

Whenever Fagan, the mentor of David Copperfield,
desired to rob successfully, he raised the cry of "stop
thief," in order to transact business and retreat safely.
So, when our "philanthropists" wish to avert our gaze
from the misery at their doors, which is of their own
making, they seek to rivet the attention of mankind
upon "the poor negro slaves" of the Southern Confederacy.   They forget, or are wilfully blind to the
fact, that "infanticide in Nottingham or Birmingham,
and SLAVERY in Manchester or Leeds," were more awful

and abominable to the humane sensibilities of Charlotte Elizabeth, than narrations of Indian, Chinese or African misery. Imagine an English or Scottish coal mine, dark as midnight, and relieved only by the flicker of the miner's lamp—deprived of a single breath of air—a subterranean charnel-house of living woe! Behold there the young wife—the yet infant daughter—girdles around their waists, with wooden cars, heavily loaded with coal, attached by iron chains thereto, and drawn by them along the seams of the mines, as if humanity were horses and asses. "But look at these unfortunates," says the *North British Review*, "the infant serfs of a *neglected* rural district! Look at them physiologically—observe their lank, colorless hair, screening the sunken eye and trailing on the bony neck; look at the hollow cheeks, the candle-like arms, and unmuscular shanks that serve them for legs"! Yes! look at these "unfortunates" first entering the appalling darkness of a coal mine at the tender age of nine, and then and there commencing their long and endless apprenticeship of misery. They rarely reach, without regard to sex, the age of twelve, before their sorry life of toil begins. In those mines they remain whole weeks, during the winter season, without beholding the sun except upon the Sabbath or some rare chance occasion. Crowded together, both sexes indiscriminately, semi-nude or totally naked—there they are with delicacy and morality dead within them.

The proportion of female children employed in the mines of East Scotland is incredibly large. They are compelled to carry coal upon their backs up steep ladders, and thus remain employed at least twelve hours out of every twenty-four. Night work is a matter of ordinary practice in those districts, and the poor children are not, unusually participants in it. Six months even of such labor is said to materially change and deform the physical structure, to injure the whole system, and to impair the mental faculties. Not five per centum of these "unfortunates" know how to read or write; and but few, if any of them, are capable of putting syllables or words respectably together. The state of education in the coal fields of Lancashire is still worse. Here there can hardly be found a collier, or a collier's child, with the slightest rudiments of learning. Indeed, throughout the coal regions of Great Britain generally, ignorance, imbecility, irreligion, profanity and immorality, are of stupendous universality. Young men and women arrive at the age of maturity without the slightest conception of the existence of a living God! They never join in prayer or go to church. They have no idea of the Saviour of man or of His mission. Some of them have never heard of Christ or His apostles, unless by accident. They do not know how to repeat the Lord's prayer; in fact, they speak their own language so barbarously as to be almost incomprehensible. They do not hold in general regard the sacredness of marriage ties. Illicit intercourse and bastardy prevail to a fearful extent in their midst. Drunkenness and crime are general amongst them. In a word, they are heathens in a Christian land, and surrounded by all the accessories of heathen misery, within call of the blatant boasts of a so-called Christian "philanthropy."

Nor is the condition of the metal workers of Birmingham, Wolverhampton, Sheffield, and the minor manufacturing places of Scotland, Worcestershire and Lancashire, less painful. Here, "in various departments of this species of manufacture, many thousands of children, of both sexes, are employed. They begin to work generally about the *eighth year;*" and they are bound to perform more than twelve hours of labor each day. The workshops in which they are placed are not unfrequently several feet beneath the earth of a damp soil; they are generally located upon unpaved back-yards, or other unfrequent places—in the dirtiest streets, in narrow courts and blind alleys—surrounded by the gutters and sewers which carry away, or are the depositaries of, the effluvia of the city. And the poor children employed in such places are mercilessly and shamelessly abused; often kicked, beaten with sticks, horsewhips and leathern straps; sometimes stricken down with the clenched fist or burned with red hot irons. Nor is the life of adults without its excruciating miseries. The grinders of cutlery are always conscious of the stealthy, but speedy approach of death. The inhalation of the dust of the grind-stone and the steel is so pernicious to their health, that they rarely average the age of thirty-five; yet these "unfortunates" are said to be opposed to the use of the dust flue, regarding with jealousy whatever increases longevity, since life is full only of sorrow and evil to them. They live in a state or drunkenness, prostitution, adultery, and godlessness—removed equidistant from the virtue of pure savageism, and the restraints of religion and civilization.

But it would be at once vain and harrowing to pursue this deplorable theme. Let it suffice to say, that the life of the collier and the metal manufacturer only fairly typifies the condition of other and various operatives. The special and general condition of those employed in the cotton factories is uniformly similar; while the same characteristics of evil and degradation pervade the whole industrial system of the British Isles—the poor lace-makers and milliners, in their garrets and cellars, included. Children, not yet seven years old, labor twelve or fourteen hours at the former business; while the sad story of the latter we will allow Sir James Clarke, one of Her Majesty's physicians, to relate. "I have found the mode of life of these poor girls," he asserts, "such as no constitution could bear. Worked from six in the morning till twelve at night, with the exception of short intervals allowed for meals, in close rooms, and passing the few hours allowed for rest in still more close and crowded apartments—a mode of life more completely calculated to destroy human health could scarcely be contrived; and at this period of life when exercise in the open air and a due proportion of rest are essential to the development of the system. Judging from what I have observed and heard, I scarcely believed that the system adopted in our worst-regulated manufactories can be so destructive of health as the life of the young dressmaker." "In the mission I have called myself to," writes Douglas Jerrold, one of the most gifted, genial, and humane of English authors, "I have stood upon the mud floor, over the corpse of the dead mother and the new-born infant— both the victims of want. I have seen a man (God's image) stretched on straw, wrapped only in a mat, resign his breath, from starvation, in the prime of life. I have entered, on a sultry summer's night, a small house, situate on the banks of a common sewer, wherein one hundred and twenty-seven human beings, of both sexes and all ages, were indiscriminately crowded. I have been in the pestilential hovels of our great manufacturing cities, where life was corrupted in every possible mode, from the malaria of the sewer to the poison of the gin-bottle. I have been in the sheds of the peasant, worse than the hovels of the Russian, where eight squalid, dirty, boorish creatures were to be kept alive by eight shillings [less than $2] per week, irregularly paid. I have seen the humanities of life desecrated in every way. I have seen the father snatch the bread from his child, and the mother offer the gin-bottle for the breast," &c., &c. And all this, alas! in *free, happy, and merrie England!* How mournful a satire, and yet a fact.

But could all this tragic misery be compared with what WE HAVE WITNESSED of woe, wretchedness, and despair in Ireland? *We* have seen there such calamities as words could not shape with raiment. *We* have seen the famishing infant seek to draw life and sustenance from the bosom of its mother's corpse. *We* have seen villages laid waste and whole townlands depopulated. *We* have looked upon the landlord apply the blazing torch to the hovel of his vassal. *We* have seen the patient stricken with typhoid fever ejected from his thatched cottage, and left to perish beneath the inclement sky of a December night. *We* have beheld the "charity of the public works" from the beginning to the ending of that accursed system. *We* have seen the peasant breaking stones, gathered by his little, naked and starving children, on the sides of the rawest and bleakest mountains, to Macadamize imaginary highways, and all for five or six pence a day. *We* have seen men and women barefooted, and for similar wages, make those roads through shaking bogs and swampy marshes, where a snipe would scorn to peck, until dropsy seized them, and their limbs became as swollen as if they had been composed of dough, and under the influence of yeast. *We* have looked upon the faces of youthful men and maidens deformed by the down of hunger and star-vation, until, like withered flowers, they dropped into premature graves. *We* have gazed upon the dead bodies of starved hundreds in the work-houses. *We* have seen the dead carried to the grave on the backs of asses, followed but by two attendants. *We* have known the churchyards to have been rifled of their prey by hungry dogs. Not the misery which makes the glory of the battle-field — not the hospital agonies which follow after—not the amputation of limbs or the removal of the devouring cancer—not what Dante saw in Male-bolge, where Ugolina wept and suffered—could compare with the potent wretchedness and despair produced by the relentless Worm of Hunger, which then gnawed the Irish heart. It was a plague not paralleled in terror and destructiveness by the plagues of Athens and of Florence. The thirst of Tantalus, which is eternal and unquenchable—the pain of Tityus, upon whose liver the vulture forever preys—were here realized upon a gigantic scale. Ireland was depopulated of two mil-lions of her inhabitants, by the retreat of the emigrant, and by the remorseless scythe of the Angel of Death; lamentations of woe were heard throughout the land, and the abominations of desolation reigned supreme.

And yet all this British and Irish misery transpired, or is still transpiring, upon the very threshold of Exeter Hall! It was within the hearing and seeing even, of her grace, the Duchess of Sutherland. But it was policy to conceal such evils. *Philanthropy* was, or is, too deeply occupied with the negro to expend any of its "charity" upon the starving white wretches, who stood, or stand, trembling, and almost lifeness, at its doors. Blind to the excruciating *slavery* that surrounds it, it sounds the tocsin of pity and sympathy on behalf of the well fed, well clothed, and well cared for, negroes of America—who, in all the relations of physical well-being and domestic happiness, are as far above the operatives of Great Britain and Ireland, as Dives was above Lazarus. With brazen effrontery, Satanic duplicity, and refreshing mendacity, in the very teeth of such appalling facts as we have above set forth, from British writers and of our known knowledge, the organ of English abolitionists—*The London Morning Chronicle*—coolly exclaims: "*The over-worked, under-fed, miserably-clad, and wretchedly-lodged [negro] slaves, have been compelled, as a means of repressing their intelligence, to work in iron collars, to sleep in the stocks, to drag heavy chains at their feet, to wear yokes, bells and copper horns; to stand naked while their masters brand them infamously, to have their teeth drawn, to have red pepper rubbed into their excoriated flesh, to be bathed in turpentine, to be thrust into sacks with mad cats, to have their fingers amputated, to be shaved, and to be whipped from neck to heels with red-hot irons.*"

Now, this is a fair and brief illustration of the . strategy of hypocrisy. The *Chronicle* has not one word of kindness, sympathy, or commisseration for the poor, "over-worked, under-fed, miserably-clad, and wretchedly-lodged" white slaves of Scotland, Lancashire, Worcestershire, and Ireland; but its indignation, wailing, and lamentations, in the cause of the American negro, outrivals the wild complaints of deserted and poisoned Philoctetes. And yet, there is not a statement—not a syllable or a word, approaching to a statement—in the synthetic quotation which we make from this anti-slavery journal, which is not a malignant, perverse, and diabolical falsehood. There is not now, and there never has been, another industrial population upon the face of this earth, better cared for or better treated—happier or more contented, in general, than the black servants of the Confederate States. They constitute a portion of the family—a part of the household gods—of their owners. In sickness or in health, in joy or in sorrow, they fly to their masters or mistresses, for sympathy and encouragement; and their appeal is rarely, if ever, made in vain. Cruel masters—men destitute of the finer feelings and sensibilities—may, and, indeed, undoubtedly do, exist; precisely as there are in all countries, and among all people, cruel parents, guardians, and master mechanics. But, as a general, almost as a universal, rule, the sympathy between master and slave is mutual, kind, and sincere. It is cemented by duty, affection, and a common dependence upon each other. But lest the slave should be subjected to mal-treatment, the law casts the mantle of its protection around him: the power of life and limb is not in the master's hands. In nine, at least, of the Confederate States, the homicide of a slave is declared murder, by statutory acts; and the slave is justified for the killing of a man in self-defence. In some of the States, if the slave satisfies the courts that he has been cruelly treated by his master, he will be granted his freedom. In others, if he is not comfortably fed and clothed, and from such usage is driven to the perpetration of theft, the master is held responsible for that which he steals. But the best bulwark of his rights is derived from social laws and usages. And so it is now, and ever has been, among all civilized peoples.

Mr. Lane informs us that the Arabs and the Turks deem it disreputable and reprehensible to set free an aged, maimed, sick, or helpless slave. "Indeed! you surely cannot be so cruel: what would become of the poor slaves if they were free!" exclaimed the Vizier of the Shah of Persia, upon being informed by the British ambassador, that his master would set free those of the Persian slaves who had fallen under his jurisdiction. Of the serfs manumitted in the Baltic provinces of Russia, Mr. Kohl says, that "formerly a noble could not, by any means, get rid of his serfs; and, whenever they were in want, *he was forced to support them.* At present, the moment a peasant becomes useless and burdensome, it is easy to dismiss him; on account of which, the serfs, in some part of the provinces, *would not accept of the emancipation offered, and bitterly lamented the freedom*, as it was called, *which was forced upon them.* The serf often mourningly complains that he has lost a FATHER and kept a *master;*" and the lord informs them, in refusing to grant their little requests, that they are *no more his children.* This feeling is permanent, sacred, and almost universal amonst the negro slaves of the American plantations. President Madison once gathered around him all of his numerous slaves. He explained to them his motives in calling them together, and offered to manumit them if they desired to be free. But they instantly and unanimously declined. They reasoned, with a sounder philosophy than their betters might have done, that they were born upon his estate—that they were attached to the locality and to their master—that in sickness or in health they had been

provided for by him, with raiment, food, and medical
care—that if set free, they would have no home to
shelter, or parental friend to protect, them—and that
since *slavery* furnished them with all that imparts happiness of life, peace, plenty, and security, they preferred
it to a nominal freedom of uncertainty, and precarious-
ness in its consequences.*

Nor was their decision either strange or unnatural.
The relations of kindness and sympathy which exist in
the Southern States between the negro and his master,
are incomprehensible to Northerners and Europeans;
and seem incredible to both. For instance, over the
very room in which these lines are written—in a second
story parlor of a Richmond, Va., mansion,—there is a
negro woman, sick of consumption, occupying the same
apartment with her mistress, attended daily by the family

---

* Since writing the above, we have perused the following notice in
the Boston *Traveller*, an organ, next in abolition influence to the New
York *Tribune*:

"THE WILL OF A FREE COLORED WOMAN IN FAVOR OF HER SON, A
SLAVE.—An aged colored woman, named Ann Jackson, died in this
city a few months since, leaving some $700 or $800 in the Savings
Bank, the accumulation of deposits made from time to time during the
past twenty-five years. She was formerly a slave at Richmond, and
leaves one son in slavery, the house-servant of a wealthy and respectable gentleman of that city. By her last will she leaves her property
to W. L. Peabody, Esq., of Lynn, in trust for the benefit of her son,
who she said did not desire his freedom, or in case of his death, for his
children. A correspondence was opened with gentlemen in Richmond,
by which it was ascertained that her son was perfectly contented, and
has a family of five or six children, slaves like himself. Assurances
were given that any money sent to 'Sam' would be scrupulously used
for his benefit, but in consequence of the present war it is deemed
best to hold on to the money for the present, and place it at interest,
in the hope that it may at no distant day be of substantial benefit to
the person for whom it was intended."

physician, and watched over with more than motherly affection and solicitude. While passing, for the first time, in the month of April, 1861, through the States of Georgia and Alabama, we accompanied a high-toned and accomplished Southern lady, attended by her negress servant, both of whom eat luncheon out of the same dish and drank out of the same silver cup; a freedom or leniency, which at that time appeared to *us* singularly strange and revolting. But we soon discovered that the child of the master and the slave were often nursed from the same bosom; we witnessed the black and white children mingle together in mutual fellowship, and build in common their mimic summer-houses and summer-gardens; and we thought how impossible it was, under such circumstances of habitual life-association, for the same feeling of repulsion toward the degraded race to exist here, which prevails and is fashionable in the Northern States.

A distinguished officer of the Confederate Army recently related an autobiographical incident, which reminded us of the discovery of Ulysses by his nurse. In infancy, he said, his mother was too feeble and sickly to nurture him, and the food of his young life was drawn from the breast of a negro slave; her own negro child being nursed upon the other breast. Having arrived at maturity, he entered the United States Navy, went to sea, and remained absent from home nine years. When he returned, he found his family at a fashionable watering place—his sister, a married woman and a mother. Ithacus-like, he did not discover himself, but entered into a conversation with the latter, which was by her regarded as painfully familiar. Meanwhile the old black nurse entered, knew him instantaneously, flung her ebony arms around his neck, and tenderly kissed him upon the lips. "God bless her," he added, "I thought more of her frank embrace than I could of the caresses of youthful and beautiful, but colder and conventional pretenders."

During the assault upon Fort Sumter a negro slave resolved to carry his young master fresh water in defiance of the enemy's fire. A citizen remonstrated, stating that "Anderson would shoot him" for his temerity. "No! no! master," was the reply, "he dare not do so, for if he did my young master *would call him to account for it.*" The confidence of this slave in the face of danger is easily accounted for, from the fact that every negro has full reliance in his master's willingness and capacity to protect him. Nor is this belief founded upon delusion. A wrong done to a slave, or an insult even offered to him, is speedily resented, and sometimes bloodily, by his owner. A few years ago the wealthiest citizen of the State of Georgia was shot, in endeavoring to avenge the wrongs, real or imaginary, of his negro servant. One of the bloodiest fights between two men that we have ever witnessed, was upon a race course in Florida, and having a similar cause for its origin and purpose.

But the kindliness with which the slave is generally treated, is best illustrated by the great distance which removes him from want or destitution. In the cities, towns and villages of the South, the slave population are better clad than the mechanics of any country in Europe. They are never found penniless like the less fortunate industrial classes of other countries; but, on the contrary, some of them have money when their superiors are without it. We have known two brother-slaves, hack-drivers in Montgomery, Alabama, to have subscribed

several hundred dollars toward the loan demanded by the
Government of the Confederate States. The negro man,
Charles, who waits upon us daily, purchased his own
freedom, and that of his wife and three children, for the
round sum of *three thousand dollars;* and although he
earns now about one thousand dollars annually, (out of
which he is necessitated to support his family) he unhesi-
tatingly regrets his error in buying his freedom. Another slave, once the property of a Richmond vintner,
paid $1500 for his freedom, and is now a " free " citizen
of Ohio, barefoot and almost shirtless, while his brother,
still a slave, is respected in Richmond, and with a Bank
account of some consideration. Now, here are two negroes, who, while held to "slavery," amassed more
money than *all* the laborers of any county in Ireland, or
shire in England, can save in a generation. He who
bought his own freedom, and that of his family, and still
resides in a slave State, earns more in one year than is
earned in two by any ordinary Northern mechanic; but
he who, having bought his freedom through the kindly
munificence of slave-owners, chose a " free " State as
his home, is now drinking the very dregs of the cup of
misery and vice.

The author—born a British subject—arrived in New
York in 1849, where he resided till the spring of 1861.
During that time the general characteristics and social
status of the negro in that State were: degradation,
laziness, theft, and extreme poverty and licentiousness.
At the South, on the other hand, he is, no matter whether
slave or free, removed from all of these vices, the latter
excepted. We know of several slaves, now employed as
porters by respectable merchants, whose honesty has
been repeatedly tested by their masters dropping at

6

night sums of money, varying in value from five cents
to twenty dollars, upon the floors which they had to
sweep in the morning, but which, in every instance, were
voluntarily restored. Perhaps, indeed, this honesty of
theirs, instead of being intuitive and founded upon absolute rectitude, is merely intellectual and the result of
cunning speculation. They have all that their hearts
could desire, suitable to their station and condition of
life. Their whims are gratified; their blunders and
idiosyncracies regarded in the light of humor, and their
gay, costly garments viewed with pride, by all, or nearly
all, of their respective masters and mistresses. And
their general intelligence is greatly underrated by those
who are unacquainted with them. We have known men
in Ireland, who did not know the English alphabet, yet
in that tongue could narrate stories and speeches from
the "Iliad" of Homer; gathered, of course, from the
lips of some village pedagogue, or (like the Arab Sheik)
itinerant prodigy who succeeded to the ancient bard, and
lived by his wit. And so of the negro slaves; there
are a large per centage of them who can "read and
write, and cipher too." They know and inculcate that
while there are idleness and starvation in the Northern
States—while stagnation of business and bankruptcy
there, throws every few years, hungry and cold, the laboring classes out of employment, fireless, foodless, clothe-
less—while long processions of poverty and sorrow-
stricken women, with their famishing infants clinging to
their milkless breasts, roam the streets of the Atlantic
cities, imploring *their masters* in vain for bread *—the

---

* The following is the recent testimony of an unkindly and unwilling
witness—an organ at present of the Northern Government—the New

blacks of the Southern States are secured in the possession of every blessing of which those unfortunate whites
are pitilessly robbed. They know and inculcate, that
while agrarianism and bread riots convulse society in the
Eastern and Northern States, their brother slaves around
them can eat, drink, dance, sing, and make merry, in
peace; as if sadness and want had flown from the earth.
In brief, whoever upon the face of this planet may hunger or thirst—may suffer for the ordinary necessaries or
conveniences of life—the negro population of America
are not of them.

Here, then, is the race—or the branch of a race,
rather—in whose name and behalf a terrible, unnatural,

York *Herald*. Speaking of destitution in the Metropolitan district of
New York, it says: "The Census Marshals return 114,966 *paupers
in the Metropolitan district, wholly or partially supported at the public
expense during the year.* Thus we see that about *one in every ten of our
population was either wholly or in part supported at the public expense.*
This is independent of a large number supported by private charity,
for which our citizens are proverbial. *The number of criminals con-
victed within the year in the Metropolitan district was* 50,958—thus showing that   *   *   *   *   *   *   *.   though freedom is
the normal condition of the white man, he drags at every step the
galling chain of inferiority in social life. Here, among one million
two hundred thousand people, *one person in every ten is wholly or in
part aided by public charity.* Would it not be better to reflect seriously
on this condition of social life before we make war on the institution
under which the physical comforts of the laboring classes are well
provided for? The fact that within the last quarter of a century the
slave population has about doubled—increased from two to four millions—shows that in physical comforts and general good treatment
they have little to complain of. *That they are happier than the free
blacks, both North and South, no one can truthfully deny; that they are
better cared for in sickness, have more of the necessaries of life, than the
great body of the laboring white class in the free States, is equally evi-
dent.*"

and devastating civil war has been fomented—reclaimed as they are, from the barbarism, not only of their origin and ancestors, but from that of their innate nature; and elevated, in the scales of moral and doctrinal Christianity and civilization, to a degree never known before to any equal number of their family. But for many long years this crusade of aggression upon the constitutional rights of the South, and of revolution in the Federal Union, has been assiduously prosecuted by the politicians and intellectual classes in the abolition section of the States. Their journals teemed with malignant vilification of the South —with studied and exaggerated misrepresentation of Southern institutions, resources, and even Christianity. The family relations, the unimpeachable virtue of females, the honor and courage of brave and heroic men— all and each formed the staple theme of Northern scurrility, libel, and wilful falsehood. Popular applause greeted the labors of the infamous slanderer; and, like the informer who measures his gains by the corpses of his victims, he advanced in popular favor in proportion as he became the successful traducer of his country. Even the most respectable publishing houses became infected with this vile disease. A few years since, all meritorious or standard literature was repulsed from their presses, and negro tales and romances, written from the stand-point of Caucasian sentimental sympathy, could only hope to meet with success. Books like "Dred," "Solomon Northrup," and "Ida May," became the fashion of the day. Publishers who but recently had been bankrupt, rose to opulence, and in one instance retired from business, upon the profits of such publications.

Yet, during the continuance of this aggressive and pragmatical carnival, crime prospered; and squalid wretch-

edness surrounded those who were sounding the trumpet
of freedom and servile insurrection in the negro's ear.
Misery, drunkenness, pollution, degradation, barbarism,
irreligiousness, lawlessness, and utter obliviousness of
shame, virtue, manliness, Briarean and Hydra-headed,
stalked forth through Anne street of Boston, and the
Five Points of New York.

Our task, however, must be performed with delicacy;
we are constrained to wear the visor of refinement; we can
neither be analytical or particular. But Mrs. Harriet
Beecher Stowe is a New England lady—one of no ordinary
intellectual endowments—like Josephus, of clerical origin;
and were it not that like him, she is also a renegade from
truth, patriotism, and humanity—might have been a phi-
lanthropist.   It is computed that from her region of the
country, there are in the city of New York alone, eighteen
thousand females—daughters of the Puritans—forever lost
to decency, womanly virtue, pure maternity, God and society.   Indeed, most of the unfortunate professional prostitutes of this great land, remarkable for their beauty and
attractions, have been turned out upon the world, seduced
victims, from the factories of New England; not one christian to be found to redeem one victim of them from this
holocaust of sin and despair !   Poor creatures ! they are
constrained to make of their own hearts the temples of
their souls' tragedies, without a commiserating word of
kindliness or hope from a cold and hypocritical world—
every one's hand against them, and, necessarily, their
hands against every one.   It was reserved for a French-
man, the younger Dumas, to effecctively raise his voice in
behalf of this class of miserables—to preach unto the cal-
lous hearts of society, the greatest sermon that has been
preached since the days of Chrysostom—through the

pages of *La Dame aux Camelias*. Mary, the sister of
Lazarus, and Mary, the Mother of God, did not despise
Mary, the Magdalene.   But, like the Pharisee who
spurned the Publican, Mrs. Stowe was blind, and deaf,
and senseless, to the living woe of her fallen New England sisters.   Yet she would not be idle; she would be
the feminine Loyola of the New Hemisphere ; but she
resolved to swim with the current ; she had not the spirit
of Athanasius, to confront and defy opinion ; her voice,
and the influence of her pen, were to be wielded in regene-
rating the already *regenerated negroes of her neighbors*.
She wrote and had published " UNCLE TOM'S CABIN."
It was a fraudulent and virulent assault upon the Southern institution of "Slavery."   It was translated into
several of the European tongues.   Amongst others, it
gave tone and relish to the Munchausenisms of the London *Chronicle*.   The Pharisaical crowd at home applaud-
ed and exalted the effort.   Henceforward the authoress
was to be ranked above Cervantes and De Foe.   " Uncle
Tom" was to be as immortal as "Robinson Crusoe."   But
the kind fidelity and obedience of *Friday* are remem-
bered ; while the supernal ethics of *Tom* are ranked with
the miraculous speeches of Balaam's ass.   *We do not
mean to be skeptical, but simply critical.*   Were it not
for the teachings of Christian Caucasian masters, the
Louisiana negro would hardly have sung religious para-
phrases of David's Psalms.   Were it not for the influence of the Angel and Balaam, it is equally doubtful,
whether the Israelitish quadruped would have outstripped
his brethren of the same species in inspiration, and uttered prophecies of supernatural import.

What, then, could have been the motive of all this,
agitation—of all these slanders—of all this belligerent

literature? We can understand why St. Columban
penetrated England and Scotland, and crossed over to
Germany and Switzerland; and why St. Francis Xavier
confronted the hostile Japanese. It was to make con-
quests under the banners of the Cross, and redeem
heathen souls. A similar holy purpose nerved French
Jesuits to explore our American forests, and brave the
dangers of famine, of the stake, and the tomahawk. But
the negroes upon behalf of whom Mrs. Stowe and her
abolition coadjutors had written, and spoken, and done
so much, were already prosperous and contented, rela-
tively civilized and christianized. If their love for this
species of mankind was exemplary, all Africa, in full and
primeval barbarism, and semi-civilized and degenerate
Hayti, Jamaica, Guiana, were open to their zeal.

The progress of the negro race in the Slave States is
remarkable and unexampled. At the era of our independence, there were in all of the thirteen original
States, composing the then Federal Union, but little
more than 600,000 slaves—twelve of these being slave
States. Of those, seven became afterward free States,
leaving out of the thirteen, to the South, but five. Yet
there is at the South to-day a slave population of between
four-and-a-half and five millions of slaves; happier and
better cared for in every physical and spiritual relation,
than any other equal numbers of industrial classes upon
the face of the globe. Nay, but the slaves are generally,
in every element of utility, respectability, and refinement, far in advance of the free negroes of the slave
States even. "As to a free negro hiring himself out for
plantation labor," writes Mr. Lewis, seventeen years
before the act of British emancipation, "no instance of
such a thing was ever known in Jamaica; and probably

no price, however great, would be considered by them as a sufficient temptation." And the same is true of the free negro everywhere. In 1839, one year after the act of emancipation, the exportation of sugar from the Island of Jamacia had fallen off 8,460 hogsheads, while the exportation of coffee, in the same year, had decreased 38,554 hundreds weight—almost one-third of the whole amount of the preceding year. Between 1846 and 1853, there were *one hundred and sixty-eight sugar estates* wholly abandoned, and sixty-three partially— valued three years after the emancipation at nearly eight and a half millions of dollars. Of coffee plantations, there were twenty partially, and two hundred and twenty-three completely, deserted ;—valued in the same year at $2,500,000; while of grazing farms, there were one hundred and thirty-two totally or partially forsaken, valued at about a million and a half of dollars—making a grand total, in seven years, of over six hundred estates, relinquished to barbarism and decay, and valued forty years ago at nearly $13,000,000. *Now*, according to John Bigelow, one of the editors of the New York *Evening Post*, "the finest land in the world may be had at any price and almost for the asking. Labor receives no compensation; and the product of labor does not seem to know how to find the way to market." Estates, which once were worth $2,000 per annum, do not now yield the value of their cultivation. The busy hum of the mills and machinery of capitalists are silenced in Jamaica. The freed negroes, in sloth and idleness, bask in the sunshine, upon what were formerly the planta- tions of their masters. While the intrepid Englishman is sacrificing his life beneath a burning sun, the negro lives by stealing, or carrying away as a matter of course, the

yams which grow spontaneously upon the plantation of
the former.   Where were formerly the race-course and
the theatre—where the city rose in pride, and happy
faces thronged the market-place—there are to-day ruin
and desolation; rats and negroes disputing their respective claims to squatter sovereignty, and nettles and ivy
ornamenting the site of public buildings.

Even British Guiana—once the garden of gardens—
has become a wild forest again—swamps and wild beasts
having taken the place of cultivation and civilized man.
All along the banks of the Demarara river, before
emancipation blossoming like the rose, and covered with
plaintains and coffee, there are now misery, desolation,
broken bridges, and impassable roads.   Essequibo, and
its once famous Arabian coast, formerly the boast of
British colonists, is now almost a desert waste.   And
the fate of Berbice is no better.   Of its 18,000 black
inhabitants, twelve thousand have degenerated to a condition of pure savageism, and withdrawn from all industrial pursuits in ignorance and idleness.   In 1829, the
district on the west bank of the Berbice river, gave employment to nearly four thousand slaves; whereas there
are hardly five hundred persons employed there now.
The whole is rapidly becoming one vast swamp; and, to
use the language of the historian, Alison: "*the negroes,
who in a state of slavery were comfortable and prosperous beyond any peasantry in the world, and rapidly
approaching the condition of the most opulent serfs in
Europe, have been by the act of emancipation irretrieva-
bly consigned to barbarism.*"

The same may be said of Hayti, once the pride of the
ocean, now a political curse and social ulcer, with the
monstrous tragedy of which the reader cannot be unac-

quainted. Robespierre, Danton, Brissot, and other blood-hounds and incarnate devils, of the French Revolution, calling themselves *Amis des Noirs*, and anticipating the Beechers, Sewards, Garrisons, Phillipses, and Parkers, of the North, stimulated the negroes of this unfortunate Island into a servile and barbarous insurrection. The atrocities which ensued are without parallel in the most diabolical annals of crime. "The victorious slaves," says Alison in his "History of Europe,"—"marched with spiked infants on their spears instead of colors; they sawed asunder the male prisoners, and violated the females on the dead bodies of their husbands." And when this demoniacal work of unutterable brutality, in the drama of Haytien "liberty" was completed—what followed? The sugar exported from this Island in the year 1789, amounted to 672,000,000 pounds. In 1806, seventeen years after, the exportation had fallen to 47,516,531 pounds. Nineteen years later, in 1825, the exportation of sugar from Hayti was 2,020 pounds, and in seven years more it had entirely ceased! Thus, by giving freedom to the Haytien negroes, in the short space of forty-three years, humanity and civilization were deprived, in the aggregate, of 28,896,000,000 pounds of sugar and the Queen-Island of the seas relinquished to barbarism, desolation, brutal licentious-ness, and crime in every hideous form. In a condition of slavery, the negro may prove himself to be a most useful, interesting, and affectionate animal; but he will not work without a master. The experiment of Joshua R. Giddings—the most generous and sincere of all American abolitionists—exemplifies this. He had a large tract of land settled by negroes, upon each of whom he bestowed a portion of it, with all of the implements necessary to the farmer. In a few years the village was deserted, the land remained waste and un-cultivated, and Mr. Giddings was constrained to confess that his black Eutopia was but a fond and idle dream.

"Oh! for the rarity of Christian charity under the sun." Mrs. Stowe labored, like Æsop's mountain, until from the depths of her great heart she brought forth "Uncle Tom;" over which the whole North, and all Europe, uttered loud lamentations, and cries of commiserating anguish, that would have put the grief of the three ladies of Bagdad to the blush. The South was anathematized, and banished from the communion table of international polity, because her plantations, like those of Hayti and the British West Indian Islands, were not turned over to ruin, decay, and primeval barrenness; and her slaves placed upon the highway of degeneracy and barbarism. It mattered not that she yielded to civilized man an annual revenue of nearly two hundred and fifty millions of dollars—imparted labor, and therefore life and happiness, to countless millions of human beings—and clothed, perhaps, one-half of the peoples of Christendom. It mattered not that in the year 1800, there were in the United States 1,087,395 free blacks, and only 893,041 slaves; while in 1851 the slave population of the Southern States was 3,204,287, and the free black population of the whole United States 434,495—of which freemen, however, the *greater moiety resided in slave States*. Before she could uncover her head, or kneel down to worship, in the Pharisee or Puritan's Temple, she was required to place upon the altar of fanaticism, her wealth, happiness, prosperity, civilization, Christianity, and humanity. In vain would she plead reason and experience. In vain would she appeal to the truths of argument. In vain would she urge, that of the fifty millions of souls inhabiting Africa, four-fifths are the slaves of each other —that the Southern slave is civilized and a christian— and, to quote the words of a talented writer, that in Africa (where the genius of our philanthropists should be exercised) "the master had the power of life and death over his slaves; that they were frequently fed, killed, and eaten, like oxen and sheep in this country; the hind and forequarters of men, women, and children, being exposed for sale in the butcher's shambles; and the living women, when not fattened for table delicacy, reduced to beasts of burden." All this could not avail: the ultimatum of the abolitionist was emancipation. Paul, the servant of Christ—he who testified his faith before Agrippa—restores the white christian fugitive slave to his white christian master, with a promise to compensate the latter for any damages he might have suffered by the absence of the runaway. The Beecher family, wiser by more than eighteen centuries, *teach the black slave to become a thief, and steal himself from his lawful owner.* The good Las Casas, Adrian V., and the followers of St. Jerome, *advocated* slavery, as the best missionary means of civilizing and christianizing the negro; but better the kraal of the savage, the barracoon, and the carnival feast, in the estimation of the abolitionist, than the contentment of the plantation and the paternity of the master's mansion. As late as the 17th century, Bossuet—the greatest of modern Divines—declared that to condemn slavery was to condemn the Holy Spirit— Christ and St. Paul; but Mrs. Stowe would doubtless regard him as speaking by inspiration of the devil, and "Uncle Tom" preferable to the Bible which so educated him. Fenelon, the kind, plastic, and benevolent Bishop

of Cambray, coincided with Bossuet, however. "Farewell "—says Minerva, in the guise of Mentor, and then
the slave of Hazael—"farewell, my dear Telemachus;
the slave who fears the gods, cannot dispense with his
obligation to attend his master. The gods have made
me the property of another; and they know that if I
had any right in myself, I would transfer it to you
alone." But the lesson of the Beechers for the slave,
on the contrary, is to give his master a long night and
bloody blanket.

And yet, oh! Beecher family, we must be pardoned
for not accepting you as our mentors, in preference to
those great and good men. The purpose for which God
created them, we can readily conceive. His motives in
imparting life to you and other troublesome insects—
mosquitoes, for instance—are hidden from our finite view,
and wrapt up in His own infinite and inscrutible wisdom.

XIV.

MANKIND are so constituted that some are honest and
consistent, while others are dishonest and inconsistent:
between whom there is naturally a perpetual struggle
for ascendancy. As in social, so in political life—the
ascendancy of evil men upon the abasement of the virtuous, will produce political disasters, or bring society to
chaos. Where virtue and integrity have forsaken the bosoms of the majority, no form of Government, however
excellent—no system of political expediency—no constitution or written codes—no artificial barriers, erected
against tyranny by the wisdom of sages, can withstand
the insidious and persistent encroachments of those who

are corrupt, and in whose hearts love of country lies dead. There, tyranny and usurpation are the substitutes of justice and moderation; usurpation, like Reynard in the garb of a pilgrim, sits mantled in the purple of the law; the favorite has the place of the patriot; and the obsequious flatterer hurls the statesman from his seat. *Obsequium amicos, veritas odium parit.* The administration of government is wrested from the hands of the trustworthy, and placed at the disposal and uncontrolled pleasure of some one man, who deals with public affairs in accordance with his agreeable caprice, and to the gratification of an army of partisan sycophants. This fortunate individual can gratify vanity and avarice—can reward obedience and subserviency, with honor, office, and emolument—and can cover the opposition of honesty with obloquy, confusion, and dismay. So long as the patriot persists in resisting the march of the tyrant over the ruins of liberty, so long he will be the target of misrepresentation, and the victim of the poisoned tooth of slander—denounced as a demagogue by the venal and the vile—and hounded even as a traitor by the yelping pack of their powerful master. But the moment he succumbs—the moment he betrays the interests of the Nation—that moment he regains his lost influence; he can become a patron and benefactor; his coffers may be enriched with spoils from off the shroud and coffin of his country. His sacrifice of popularity is rewarded with the traitor's purse, and his mission henceforward is to educate the people to relinquish liberty and acquiesce in political profligacy. Who can doubt the truthfulness of this photograph? Let the skeptic reflect upon the fate of such patriots as Breckinridge, of Kentucky, and Vallandigham, of Ohio, in the late Congress of the United

States. They manfully resisted the usurpation, and opposed the unconstitutional aggressions, of the sectional
tyrant; they were, in return, subjected to the tortures of
vilification, insult, outrage, and vulgar abuse. Were
they formed of such clay as the recreant Richardson, of
Illinois, or the base Scott, who, like Athenian Hippias,
endeavored to enslave his mother State, they would have
been rewarded by the grimaces of Lincoln's Court, and
the fulsome adulations of the general herd: for virtue
had forsaken the hearts of the people in that section of
our land. The United States had, but a few months previously, a Constitution and a Form of Government,
which were wont to be the boast of 30,000,000 of freemen, the admiration of the civilized world, the day-dream
of hope to the oppressed nationalities, and the stumbling
block of kings and tyrants. But the men of the North,
maddened by a pampered prosperity, and impatient of
rivalry, eschewed justice and rectitude, refused to grant
their partners of the Federal system political equality,
and proud in their strength of numbers and in the asser-
tion of an iniquitous abstraction—they trampled upon
the Constitution and set the laws at defiance; elected a
President pledged to ruin the interests and to confiscate
the property of one section of the country; rejected all
measures of compromise, concession, or conciliation; insulted and misrepresented the minority, while violating
their legally guaranteed rights; and, finally, waged a
war of subjugation and extermination, against a people
whom they claimed to be still their fellow-citizens—their
natural allies—their kindred of blood and lineage—and,
surely, their best patrons and supporters. Having been
long, and we may add, justly, deprived of the administration of public affairs—pregnant with avarice, and

hungering for office and patronage, they beat the rounds of every wind of doctrine in political chance, and triumphed at length upon a platform of anti-slavery fanaticism. Before they had thus succeeded in the elevation of Mr. Lincoln to the Presidency, they had, for more than twenty-five years, encroached, in many outrageous forms, upon the sovereign independence of the Southern States. The Federal Constitution rendered the restoration of fugitive slaves a moral and political duty; the Northerner observed this injunction by *robbing the slave-owner and stealing away the slave*—all in the name and for the greater glory of God! Singularly enough, the parents of these moralists—who teach the negro the unapostolic christianity *of stealing himself*—were those who stole from their homes, and sold for the highest penny, the Angola ancestors of our present slaves. They grew wealthy and powerful by the gigantic commerce, and notwithstanding that, by international law, this traffic has been declared piracy, their offspring still cling to the profitable practice. The slavers which prowl along the coasts of Guinea, are Northern or New England ships, manned by Northern or New England *pirates*. There is not one of these vessels which lands her human cargo in the coves or corners of Cuba or Florida, that is not owned by a Puritan abolitionist. Having placed the price of his victims to the credit of his account, he seeks to whitewash himself in sight of Heaven and man, by endeavoring to rob the purchaser of the very goods which he had himself previously sold to him; realizing the poet's picture of the hypocrite:

> "———— with one hand he put
> A penny in the urn of *charity*,
> And with the other took a shilling out."

There is nothing easier, in this world, than for duplicity to screen its own iniquity, beneath the assumed envelope of philanthropy,—always worn by the transgressor at the expense of others. The abolitionist has ever been, and is now, in so far as the system can be clandestinely practised, the decoyer, the importer, the seller, of the negro; the Southerner is his owner, civilizer, christianizer—his best friend, his adopted parent, his guardian by force of interest and duty. Of his relations toward the slave the latter is proud; the former ashamed, even unto sensitiveness. Social proscription is, as it ever has been and will be, the fate of the slave-trader; but to avoid this odium, the Northerner, like Saturn, would devour those upon whom he was the first to place the manacles of bondage.

The partner, however, if not the teacher, of New England in the slave trade, was Old England; precisely as both have recently been partners in their aggressive and inconsistent anti-slavery crusades. Toward the close of the reign of Elizabeth, the full value and utility of the negro was discovered.

England, with much to boast of that is grand and glorious in the history of liberty, has her escutcheon tarnished by deeds of gross injustice, and unrivalled iniquity. While tenacious of the freedom of her own immediate children, she deprived the other peoples who had the misfortune to fall under her sway, of this precious right. Even the inhabitants of the counties palatine of Durham and Chester, within her own borders, were once oppressed by her as aliens and enemies. For more than two hundred years, she treated Wales as a conquered province. Her career in Scotland was long a career of cruel wrong, rapine, and carnage.

7

And seven centuries of blood, persecution, and sculptured tyranny, have ineffaceably fixed the traces of her fangs upon that ghastly ghost, commonly called "the Irish Nation." The vain attempt to inaugurate a similar policy upon this continent, stripped her haughty diadem of its fairest and most precious jewel; but ere we had separated ourselves from her, she had imparted to us the institution of African servitude.

It is, indeed, true, that the importation of negro slaves to the new world was first instituted by Spain; but in adopting the policy, the motives of England were entirely different—were altogether selfish and commercial. Spain, while enslaving the African, was bent upon christianizing and civilizing him; of benefiting him and alleviating the condition of his betters. The pious Las Casas saw the Indians perish—melting away, in fact, from the face of the earth, beneath the yoke of bondage;—and combining the qualities of a statesman with his attributes of a Christian divine, he recommended the importation of negroes, as being naturally and physically better suited to the labor and climate of the South. He urged, too, that *this was the only feasible plan* whereby their barbarous heathenism could ever be brought under the dominion of the Cross; and in this opinion the Hyeromite monks and the Cardinal Tortosa, are said to have coincided. Forthwith the African slave trade became a recognized and lucrative branch of Spanish commerce.

But England, under the enterprising rule of Elizabeth (into whose heart pity or remorse never found entrance, while self-interest stood in the way), profiting by the discovery, outrivalled Spain in the traffic, and built upon it nearly all of her present wealth and ascendancy.

During a period of two hundred and seventy-four years, she was the most famous negro catcher that the world had ever seen; having reduced over five millions of them to slavery. In little more than one century—from 1702 to 1807—she had millions of them imported into the Island of Jamaica alone. Upon the head of every slave, so imported, she had laid a specific duty; varying from *five shillings*, in 1719, to *five pounds* about the year 1774. It is estimated that the revenue which she directly derived from the slave trade, amounted to the enormous sum of $3,600,000,000! And throughout her *brilliant* career in the prosecution of this "peculiar," but golden branch of commerce, the merchants of New York, Rhode Island, and Massachusetts, so far as their means and capacities would admit, zealously emulated her example; until, at length, they were enabled by its profits, directly and indirectly, to cope in wealth and enterprise with the parent State. The Congress of the United States, however, interposed, and—whether wisely or unwisely it matters not now, but certainly in obedience to a then prevailing sentiment of "humanity"—prohibited the continuance of the slave trade from and after the year 1808. It may, in this connection, be worth while to observe, that this measure was sustained by the representatives of Southern States; but strenuously opposed by those of New England States. Meantime, the British colonists of Jamaica became clamorous and rebellious. They were not scant of black labor-power, and they sternly protested against the oppressive duties placed by the mother country upon the imported negro. These circumstances, and the powerful sentiment of opposition to slavery at home—which finally resulted in the complete ruin of Jamaica, Dominica, and

Antigua—induced England to follow the example of our (then) own Government.

But Britain would not be idle. She would have new dominions. She would have other slaves. She fixed her gaze on India. The work of conquest and subjugation began, and 200,000,000 of human beings were ground to earth. In the short space of seventy-three years she stripped unfortunate India of $200,000,-000,000! And it is upon this enormous sum, added to the great wealth wrung from the body of the negro, that the pillars of her supreme power among the nations rest to-day.

The participation of Southerners in the slave trade was purely negative. They simply purchased negroes of those who imported and sold them. They necessarily became their owners, directors, and protectors. When American Independence was established, the white population of the thirteen States then composing the Federal Union, was *three millions;* and the servile population more than *one half-million.* But beneath the benign influence and fostering care of indulgent masters, the quota of this latter number which belonged to the six Southern States of the old Confederacy, have so increased and multiplied, as to show a population in the South, at present, of between *four and five millions of slaves* *—valued at more than $4,000,000,000 :

---

* The negro, no matter whether bond or free, prospers and increases at the South much better than he does in the North. Thus: In 1790 there were, all told, 68,080 negroes at the North; 32,635 free, and 657,047 slave in the South. In 1850, in the eighteen Free States, there but 196,994 blacks; while in the fifteen Slave States there were 238,737 free and 3,204,051 slaves—making in all, at the South, a negro population of 3,442,788.

The inconsistency of the vendors of the nucleus of all this great property, in making war upon the vendees for holding it, is only paralleled in impudent wickedness, by their greed for increase of wealth through the profits of its labor.   For it is not extravagant to assert—it is truthful to the very letter—that there is not now, and that there never has been, an equal number of industrials upon the face of this planet, whose habitual employments have so largely contributed to the commerce and riches of mankind—the produce of whose labor is so indispensable in supplying the necessary wants of the human family—and upon whom the employment, sustenance, and principal hopes of life and well-being, of so many millions of souls imperatively depend, as upon the African slave population of America—represented, at the North, in its institutional characteristics, as immoral, infamous, inhuman !   But do moral men hire their mansions to be used as brothels ?   Or do they love to fatten upon the wages of prostitution ?   While the agency of the planter in the slave is to feed, clothe, and shelter him, the English and Northern abolitionists peddle the produce of his labor throughout the four quarters of the globe ; thus enhancing the value of slavery whilst decrying it, and anointing their consciences with the jackal's share of the profits.   By mechanical discoveries and contrivances, they have helped to enlarge the area of Slavery and to make it perpetual as an institution.   The invention of the cotton-gin in America, and of the cotton-jenny in England, increased the value of the negro slave, and opened to the white man vast avenues of industry, leading to wealth and security—harmonizing, it may be said, free and slave labor.   Before the cotton-gin was invented, to clean a pound weight of cotton was esteemed the daily labor of a single hand; but by means of this ingenious contrivance, a similar hand can now clean 350 pounds in the same length of time. And so, previously to the inventions of Watt and Hargrave, and the improvements thereon of Arkwright and Crompton, one white man could clean for the cards one pound of cotton, another card it, and a third work one spindle; now, one man can clean each day 360 pounds, another card that quantity, and a third work 2200 spindles.

The various uses to which the produce of slave labor is converted by civilized nations, the moneys derived from it, and the souls that are dependent upon it, almost border upon the infinitude of numbers. It is estimated that there are in England between five and six millions of human beings who derive their livelihood from cotton alone. The slave has kept thirteen hundred mills in operation in that country, and employed there a capital of nearly three hundred millions of dollars—upon the continuance of which, the safety of the whole social fabric, and the prosperity of England, depends. In one century he has added more than two millions to the population of Lancashire. He puts in motion over 2500 factories, causes about 30,000,000 of spindles to hum the music of industry, and gives work to some 210,000 horse-power looms. France and Germany are also patrons of the slave and partakers of slave-labor; and the quantity of cotton yarn, and cotton manufactured goods, exported to India, China, Egypt, and Turkey, by England alone, show how much the ancient East depends upon this Southern institution. Great Britain exports annually to other countries, (the raw material having been a philanthropic contribution of slave-labor towards the clothing of mankind,) in the vicinity of 2,500,000,000 yards of plain and dyed manufactured cotton goods. The cotton crop of America will vary from four millions, to four millions five hundred thousand bales, per annum; and after deducting from this a sufficient quota for home wants, the remainder will yield to its owners in ready cash, at least $200,000,000.

So much for slavery and civilization.

But this is not all. It is but a mere iota of what slavery—the ramifications of which are manifold—does for mankind. The cotton plant, which may be termed the adopted child of the slave, is the most indestructible product of Nature's bosom. From the moment that it is placed out of the hands of those who sow and pick it, its mission becomes mercifully universal, hopeful, and vital—imparting employment to untold millions of operatives in every diversity of labor—opening fresh channels for the investment of capital and the circulation of money—keeping society from chaos and giving stability to governments—covering exposed nakedness from the blasts of winter and the heat of summer—saving from bankruptcy, ruin, or starvation, merchants, bankers, ship-chandlers and ship owners; the common carrier; the loaders and unloaders of cargoes; sailors; carders; spinners; weavers; engineers; mechanics; chemists; dyers; shopkeepers; tailors; sewers; lace-makers; milliners; dress-makers; rag-gatherers; paper manufacturers; printers; editors; publishers; and so on, *ad infinitum*. And yet this is but a single product of slave labor. Of rice, sugar, tobacco, etc., we have said nothing. In the State of Louisiana alone, according to Mr. Kettell, there are annually produced 362,296 hogsheads of sugar, 6,327,882 bushels of corn, and 4,911,680 pounds of rice. The total value of sugar exported to the Northern States, and other foreign countries, exceeds $31,000,000. . The revenue derived by France and England from tobacco is computed at $40,000,000.

Hercules, the benefactor, cleaned out the Augean stables, and slew the Lernæan hydra, among other deeds of the celebrated twelve labors proposed to him by Juno and Eurystheus. But the enterprises of the son of Jupiter are dwarfed by the tasks set unto themselves by the abolitionists; with Lord Brougham at their head in England, and William H. Seward in America. Four hundred millions of dollars worth of property must be destroyed to conciliate the Furies that feed upon their panic-stricken consciences. If their assumed philanthropy were genuine and founded upon self-sacrifice— if their people were ready to yield up the principal, with interest, derived by them from the slave trade, for the liberation of the slave—if themselves and their constituents were even willing to pay the owners of slave property the fair net valuation for the unparalleled sacrifice—if they were prepared to show from ascertained and unquestionable facts, how humanity and civilization would be benefited by such a radical policy— and if they could satisfactorily prove to us, that a provision of safety and usefulness was reserved for the emancipated slave—we could not refuse to respect and admire doctrines which we are now constrained to term, the vicious dreams of a cruel and heartless fanaticism. No such concessions, however, find favor with them. They are to be permitted to revel in their equivocally begotten wealth, while the slave-holder must part with his all, or consent to have his territory hemmed around with a "wall of freedom;"—which signifies the destruction of his property by means of *sanctified* robbery.

The helpless emancipated slave is to be deprived of a home, comfort, and the parental guardianship of a master; he is destined to represent once more upon earth the son of Hagar, without a friend and without a meal. The plantations which now grow golden harvests are to retrogress to their pristine condition of barren wildness. The cotton mills, and factories, and manufactories, and operatives, of Europe and America, are to stand idle or starving—all for the glory of the negro! Civilization and progress must rein their proud career, and wend a backward course; and men and women must return to the domestic and political economy of patriarchal ages! Such is the incongruous philosophy of the abolitionist; ambiguous as the blind policy of Samson, who murdered himself in order to murder others.

It has long been the ambition of the statesmen and philanthrophic pragmatists of Great Britain, to procure cotton for their market from some other source than America. With this view, they have ransacked China, India, Egypt, and Africa. Their desire in this respect, resulted, however, from an envious jealousy of the rapid growth and power of the late United States, rather than from any sincere affection for the negro. In a debate in the House of Lords, anti-slavery philosophy ventilated its real and hidden motives. The Bishop of Oxford piously revealed to his noble compeers, that the best way of putting an end to the slave-trade and successfully cultivating cotton in Africa, was to teach " the African chiefs that the employment of their *dependent* people [a delicate term, surely, for the most barbarous slavery] in the production of the *raw material* of cotton, would be more *advantageous* than the SELLING of them into slavery for transportation into *other parts* of the world." The evangelical legislator evidently recognizes cotton as a kind of tangible and indispensable fact. But since it is impossible to grow the necessary supply of it without forced or slave-labor, he considers it better that its cultivator should be the "dependent people" of some swarthy savage heathen, rather than the Christian servants of an American planter. What is sin in the latter becomes virtue in the former; the one receiving the benediction of Oxford for the very deed which earns anathema for the other. Since there are to be slaves at all, why let them be the chattels of any body but an American; and in that case even, they must religiously refrain from producing other than "the raw material," so as not to interfere with British manufacturers or British labor. And then, to accomplish this, the astute Divine appeals to the cupidity of the black chiefs; setting forth that it would be much more "advantageous" for them to reap for *themselves* the harvest of slave-labor than to allow *others* to do so: thus showing that slavery is not a wrong *per se*—is not a universal wrong—is a wrong merely attaching to the slaveholders of superior caste.

The Bishop of Oxford may be a very learned and a very holy man; but not having the examples of Anthony of Thebes or Simon Stylites before his eyes, the way of his godliness is through the highroads of wealth and luxury. It is in the splendid palace, surrounded by works of art and lighted by brilliant chandeliers, and not in a wild cave or upon a lonely pillar, that he meditates and prays. To impart zest to his devotions, his apostolic feet must press the downy carpet; the soft embroidered cushion must embrace his bended knees; the light of Heaven should fall in softened rays upon his brow, through the various devices of richly fabricated window-curtains; the richest garments, ornamented with the most seductive looking lace, must robe the limbs of his daughters, and prettily printed dresses add comeliness to their maids; and his sermons and salutations, it would be blasphemous not to have recorded upon the neatest paper. But all these necessary accessories to religion in this representative of Peter and Paul, may, alas! be produced from the "raw material" of American cotton. And hence Asia and Africa are invoked.

Admitting for fact the supposition—leaving wholly out of view the dearth of moisture in the east, but without the requisite portion of which cotton cannot be successfully grown—would the culture of this precious plant in these countries, benefit the anti-slavery cause? Or would it injure the American planter, by depreciating the value of his slaves and plantations?

It is a well-established and an indisputable fact, founded upon reason and experience, that prosperously to cultivate cotton, the planter must, at all times and seasons, have absolute *command* of labor: for of all other products, it requires the most tender and unabated care, if it would be successfully produced. The land, from which it is intended it shall be grown, must undergo a perfect system of preparation. It must be bedded up early in the winter, so as to allow the frost to pulverize the soil. It must be ploughed deeply and thoroughly, and remain unbroken between the furrows. A fine system of drainage should prevail, with a looseness of soil, to enable the roots of the plant vigorously to penetrate the earth. All stalks, grass, and vegetable matter, ought to be rolled into the ploughed furrows, to rot as a nucleus of manure. Even when all this is accomplished, heavy rains and baking winds, too frequently cake the surface of the soil; then the crust must be broken by a complete process of harrowing.

Such preparations having been consummated, the cotton seed should be sown between the 15th of March and the 15th of April, but to insure vigor to the plant, the seed should have been well saved, and at least one year old. When sown, the seed ought to be carefully covered, especially in stiff lands. As the seeds commence to crack the earth, in germinating, the cotton ridges must be artistically scraped with notched sticks. The growth of grass and all extraneous matter, with the plant, should be jealously watched and prevented. When the third leaf of the stalk appears, the soil around it ought to be ploughed with a Mississippi scraper. In about a week afterward, the "chopping" process becomes requisite—arranging the cotton into uniform stands of three or four stalks each. This is followed, in time, by another method of ploughing; whereby a sweep is at the bottom and a mould-board next to the plant—the object being to "dirt" the young plant. The bed must, however, be kept carefully up by the help of a turn plough. Afterwards it will become necessary to reduce the stalks to two in a stand, and in some lands, to one stalk. All subsequent ploughing except in extraordinary seasons, is done with the sweep and mould-board; always, of course, keeping the furrows drained; for in wet seasons the most assiduous and persistent care of the young plant becomes necessary.

As to the first picking season, that begins when the hand can pick about fifty pounds a day. This must be promptly and skilfully attended to, in order to prevent evaporation of the oil by the sun, wind, or rain. When the crop is good, cotton is picked free from leaves and

other extraneous matter; not so, however, when the
crop is short; this care is deemed then unprofitable for
apparent reasons.   Cotton seed is usually saved from the
second picking.   Then comes ginning, which must be
carefully done and at moderate speed.   Next ensues
packing; which should be avoided in dry or windy
weather, but carefully attended to in moist seasons to
secure the retention of its oil.   The bale being formed,
it should be completely enveloped in a loose bag, allowing
room for its expansion; and then bound with ropes.
When all this is accomplished—when the cotton crop of
one year is saved—it is full spring-time to commence
preparations for the next.

Now, it must be perfectly apparent to the most obtuse
understanding, that a plant requiring so much care and
attention, and almost a whole year of culture, *can never
be profitably produced otherwise than by slave labor*—by
that system, which gives to the planter absolute *control*
in directing the laborer.   No matter how indigenous
cotton may be to the soil, or however genial the sun
and clime, without this it cannot be grown in sufficient
quantities to meet the demand of civilization.   And this
fact is apparent to English statesmen.*   They have
been reluctantly compelled to recognize it.   A com-
mittee of inquiry, appointed by the House of Com-
mons, reports that it can be successfully cultivated in
certain British possessions—*with the aid of steady*

---

* "British statesmen know that all the labor in British India is
forced labor, and that whosoever has to employ Eastern laborers anywhere, must, in one form or other, *force* them to work by personal
coercion.   The Indian *ryots* labor for the English, in the production
of indigo and opium, under the cat-o'-nine-tails, the pincers, and the
kittee."—JOHN MITCHELL.

labor; and his Grace of Oxford recommends the black chiefs of Africa, to employ their *"dependent"* people in producing it. If, then, England is ever destined to compete with America in the cultivation of cotton, she must adopt the policy of *forced labor* in the exercise of public economy. *The area of slavery will thus become extended; inferior races will be controlled in the West and far off East, by Caucasian* intellect;* civilization must advance by force of such influence; and the heresies of anti-slaveryism be buried in oblivion. Britain will be constrained to return again to the point from which she started, and erred in starting.

Now, if we will suppose that this system of labor is fully established in Egypt, Africa, India, and China— all cotton-growing countries;—if we will suppose their labor-power fully disciplined in the culture of the plant, by the *necessary experience* of at least twenty-five or thirty years; and, finally, if we will suppose that the results of the vast experiments in all these countries, are great successes—how far would this be injurious to the

---

* The Caucasian can never cultivate cotton successfully. The delicacy of his structure and organization render him incapable of enduring open-field labor beneath a burning sun. He soon falls the victim of malaria in climates where the cotton plant flourishes, if subjected to the labor for which the inferior races of man seem indigenous. For instance: "the negroes are so seldom afflicted with the yellow fever," says Dr. Mosely, "that they have often been said not to be susceptible of it; and there have been instances which, under a very general prevalence of the complaint, not one has fallen sick. On other occasions some have been seized with this fever, but the number has been small, and they have recovered more easily than the whites." This disease is inflammatory, produced by external causes in hot climates, to which the organism of the negro is inured, but that of the Caucasian foreign. To the latter, it is generally fatal.

prospects and well-being of the cotton planters of the Southern Confederacy?

It is an axiom of natural, no less than of political, economy, that the normal consequence of production is consumption. China, India, Egypt, Turkey, Africa, Nubia—in brief, the whole East—embraces a population of more than 800,000,000 of souls; requiring cotton in all of its manifold uses. They are, *en masse*, sorely in need of nourishment, civilization, and some lever of progress. To make cotton a staple product of their soil, would be taking an infinite stride in this humane direction. In its culture and manufacture, the natives would have to be employed, and in proportion as their industry would be stimulated, their ingenuity directed, and their zeal rewarded, their necessities would increase, until they should at length enter the great Olympic race of human competition, as consumers, with Americans and Europeans. Commerce, Christianity, and civilization, after long ages of poverty and benighted barbarism, would dawn again upon the starving East—the cradle of humanity, where the sun of enlightenment first arose, and gradually irradiated the West with its rays. The world's immense market would be augmented; human intercourse enlarged; homogeneity made universal. But, instead of supplying Europe with the raw material of cotton, the demand for it in the East would become so great, that America would be called upon to supply the want. The Eastern hemisphere would need not only all the cotton that it could produce, but much more, perhaps, than we could supply it with. Instead of being our rival, it would become our best customer.

India and China are so densely populated, as to contain a more numerous population, upon every square

mile of their territories, than there is contained upon
any other equal portions of the earth.   Hence, the allot-
ments of their lands devoted to the production of food,
must always infinitely exceed that reserved for the culture of the cotton plant—rendering it vain for the world
to expect a sufficiency of this staple from these countries.   As we have previously seen, they even now import
annually from Europe, more pounds of *manufactured*
cotton than they are enabled to export.   The quality of
their cotton is inferior, and can never be made to approach, in points of excellence or utility, to that grown
in America.   While it grows wild and natural in many
parts of India, China, and Africa—and of course is susceptible of improvement—while the soil is often richer
in those countries than it is with us; the climate is
adverse.   In the Eastern latitudes, low enough for the
production of cotton, while at particular periods of the
year they are visited by very heavy rains, at other and
more important seasons, they are attended by continual
and unrelieved drought—these seasons being those when
the plant most needs the nourishment of moisture.
Hence the .cotton of the East is short, fuzzy, yellow-
tinged, and woolly; fitted only for the *woof* of cloth,
and, in the English market, worth little more than one-
half what American Upland cotton readily commands.*

---

* Some idea may be formed of the utility of Asiatic and other
cottons, from the following statistics, gathered from a correspondent
of an American journal:

"The quantity of cotton from India, Egypt, &c., is of a harsh,
hairy nature, and can only be spun into a thick, hard, twisted yarn,
for heavy goods, and is *not adapted to a fifth part of the trade of England, any more than so much straw.* The British cotton interest, with
Government aid, is engaged in an earnest effort to obtain supplies of

The fall of rains in Alabama, Louisiana, Georgia, Arkansas, and Mississippi—during the four seasons of the year—as shown in meteoric tables, are: In the Spring 15 inches; in the Summer 20; in the Autumn 12; and in the Winter 18—a phenomenon which, in all the other countries of the globe producing cotton, cannot be discovered: so that, when the Eastern planter would be compelled artificially to irrigate his land, the American may feel himself necessitated to drain *his* crop. Consequently, the cotton of the latter has never been excelled; neither can it be. It is suited to every variety of manufacture; but the mission of Indian and Chinese cotton is limited—twenty-five per centum of which being as much as can be used in the manufacture of fine cloths.

Yet, did none of these disadvantages exist—if the East were as naturally irrigated as our own South— if the quality of cotton produced by the former were equal to that of the latter—there would still remain obstacles in the path of the East, which would render the South mistress of rivalry. The length of voyages

---

cotton from India, Syria, Egypt, Africa, and the West Indies. In order to show the amount of the deficiency that is to be supplied from new sources, I give the following accurate returns of consumption and supply from 1842 to 1860, as made by the Manchester Chamber of Commerce. The total consumption for 1843 was 1,682,982 bales of 400 pounds each, of which the United States supplied 1,436,846, and all other countries 246,135. The total consumption of 1852 was 2,324,461 bales, of which the United States supplied 1,914,076 bales, and all other countries 410,385. The total consumption in 1860 was 3,477,458 bales, of which the United States supplied 2,797,726, and all other countries 687,732. The increased consumption of cotton in Great Britain from 1840 to 1860 was 1,794,476 bales, or over 100 per cent. of the whole consumption on the former year."

to India, China, or Egypt—the expense of freightage and insurance—the distance that cotton would have to be carried from the plantation to the sea-port, and the dearth of steamboats and railroads on the routes—would soon become too expensive for the *trade*-philanthropy of abolitionism. The freight upon every pound of cotton, now transported from America to England, rarely exceeds one cent; whereas the freight upon a similar weight, brought either from Shanghai or Calcutta, would certainly not fall short of twice that amount. Voyages from the latter ports will certainly average four months, while from the Confederate States they will not exceed three or four weeks. Thus, the whole expense of a pound of cotton, imported to England from us, will be about three cents; while, if carried from China or India, it will more than double this. Consequently, and at this rate of expenditure, the cotton which ordinarily brings 12 cents in the English market, when it would yield to the Eastern planter but *four cents*, must yield *nine* to the American.

It is not, then, the philosophy of the latter to fear the former. The true American, as a statesman, humanitarian, and Christian, would applaud the success of his would-be rival. Even if it were possible or feasible—and not outside the pale of reason and experience—he would regard it equally absurd to suppose that the sewing machine had ruined the happiness of the seamstress—that the reaping machine had destroyed the independence of the harvest-laborer—or that the cotton-gin and cotton-jenny had blighted his own fortunes—as to contemplate with jealousy the enterprise of his Asiatic competitor. He feels that every new invention made in the mechanic arts; and every fresh staple of

universal use, extracted from the womb of the soil, increases the wealth of mankind, and instead of diminish-
ing, adds to the happiness of our species, by enlarging
the matter of consumption.   The most penetrating
regret, however, that he experiences, arises from a painful consciousness that abolitionism is not actuated by a
spirit of Christian philosophy, religion, or philanthropy.
He knows that it is hatred and envy of him, which impel
the peoples of Europe and the North, to make voyages
of exploration in search of new and rival cotton regions.
If by exploring the whole earth, they could discover for
themselves elsewhere, the necessary supply of this precious and indispensable product, their ambition would
be crowned; but more especially so, if the Southern
planter should become thereby a hopeless bankrupt.
It is not love, but hate, that inspires their zeal.   And
surely—in lands of Bibles, Bible-readers, missionaries,
and tractarians—this is reversing the Divine precept of
Christ—returning evil for good—since the assailed victim has been their meek and great benefactor.

XV.

IT is related that Niobe, daughter of Tantalus, and wife to Amphion, King of Thebes, was blessed by Fortune with all the gifts of Nature and every attribute of happiness; from the enjoyment of which she was, however, debarred, by her presuming pride and arrogance. Puffed up with vain-glory and self-conceit, she jealously envied, and professed to despise, Latona, the beautiful favorite of Jupiter—disturbed her religious sacrifices, and boastfully vaunting that her own virtue, wealth, beauty and bounty were unrivalled—proclaimed that the personal charms of her children surpassed those of gods and goddesses. At length her conduct enraged Apollo and Diana—children of Latona—and they resolved to revenge the injuries of their mother, by the humiliation and punishment of Niobe. So, before her eyes, they shot with celestial arrows, first her sons, then her fair daughters, and lastly her husband; upon beholding which, Niobe swooned with grief and despair, and ere recovery could come to her, she was metamorphosed into marble, from which bitter tears forever flow.

The myth of Niobe and Latona is partially, but painfully, symbolical of the relations which have heretofore existed between the South and the North—long patience and endurance, characterizing the history of the former; haughty vindictiveness and outrages, that of the latter. The North was great—artificially; splendidly grand—but in borrowed plumage. Into her lap the whole world poured surprising contributions of wealth, exalting her luxury and perfecting her happiness. All vessels, bound to or from her harbors, and whose whitening canvas sported with the Nereides of the deep, were obsequious missionaries of her rapidly increasing beauty and splendor. Her people increased and multiplied like the promised seed of Abraham—like the stars in the firmament, or the sands upon the beach. Her cities arose out of the wilderness, so rapidly and so magnificently, as to recall the magic miracles of Aladdin's lamp. Banks, insurance offices, and monopolies flourished beneath her ægis. Stage-coaches, steamboats, and railroads, cumbered her wide domains. Her finest commercial emporium rivalled in magnificence and prosperity, as well as in crime and licentiousness, the most famous capitals of antiquity. A mighty current of treasure, surpassing that of golden Pactolus, added daily to the increasing glory of her diadem. From the tobacco plantations of Virginia and Tennessee—from the flowery and fruitful regions of Opelousas—from the sugar lands of Attakapas—from the silver shores of the Mississippi, perfumed by groves of orange and citron—from Alabama and the Carolinas, where the cotton-tree waves its kingly crest in Autumn's zephyrs—from the rich rice fields of the blessed Sea-Island coasts—from a whole Southern Empire of perpetual summer, where the princely prairies and grand savannahs are carpeted by the love-lavish hand of Flora, and over which bend the bluest of heavens—flowed the river of life, which imparted progress, and pomp, and brilliancy to the North. TWO HUNDRED AND THIRTY-ONE MILLIONS OF DOLLARS was the annual dowry which the South generously cast at her feet. More faithful to what she esteemed a patriotic duty, than that bird which is said to feed her young with her life-blood, this South drained her breasts

of untold treasures, to glut the thankless rapacity of her
enemy. She consented yearly to the payment of THIR-
TEEN MILLION OF DOLLARS, as a bounty toward the encouragement of Northern fisheries; EIGHT MILLIONS of
which went into the abolition coffers of Massachusetts.
She constituted the North her common carrier, and paid
THIRTY-SIX MILLION OF DOLLARS in requital of the service. She paid EIGHT MILLIONS, and more, annually,
for the shoes of her slaves; and over SIXTY MILLIONS
for dry goods, furniture, fish, and other commodities.
The wealth of the South being solid rather than artificial, in 1857–8—during the terrible American crisis—she
had $35,000,000, in specie, more in her banks than there
was at the North, with which she promptly came forward
to save the latter from pending ruin. But in proportion
as she scattered favors, new exactions were demanded
of her. Her sons had laid their heads to rest in love,
down in the lap of a Delilah, and they arose from their
slumber almost shorn of their strength. Her people consented to have themselves taxed at the rate of twenty-
four per cent. for the carpet upon which they stepped—
for the apparel which they wore—for the china-ware of
their households—for the mirrors and window hangings
of their parlors—for the cutlery of their pockets and
their tables—for the chairs upon which they sat—and
for the boots and shoes which they wore—all for the
self-sacrificing purpose of encouraging Northern manufacturers, and offering a premium to Northern ingenuity.
They taxed themselves, or consented to be taxed, for the
books they bought, and for the paper upon which they
wrote. They were taxed at the rate of thirty per
centum for the cigars they smoked—for the wines which
they drank—and for the pianos of their wives and

daughters—in order to stimulate Northern inventions, quackery, and cunning. The South bestowed upon the North a whole empire of territories—freely bestowed them, cheerfully, gracefully, and without murmur—notwithstanding that they were to become Free States, and, necessarily, antagonistic forces. In addition, she helped to widen the rivers, to improve the harbors, to build the light-houses and custom-houses of the North; indeed, the full measure of her generous devotion toward the aggrandizement of a false and ingrate sister, is incalculable, and will ever remain among the unwritten stories of the marvellous.

But how did the North repay all this munificence—all these splendid and princely favors—all such bountiful and prodigal benefits? Much as the infidel wife, of the Arabian tale, returned the loving confidence of the young king of the Black Isles. She was his kinswoman. He had profusely scattered upon her the treasures of his possession. Every wish of her heart was studiously and spontaneously gratified. Their connubial bliss seemed unclouded, and Love's warm blandishments added new charms to their happiness, for a brief term of years. But at length—and when too late—the unhappy prince discovered that the wife of his soul delighted in him no more—discovered that she was a traitor to his bed and enamored with a BLACK. Even when her crime was discovered, and her monster paramour's life saved by magic only—instead of reforming and repenting, she had herself arrayed in garments of sorrow—erected a mausoleum, called by her the "Palace of Tears," where she daily bewailed the stupefaction of her sable idol—but still nestled in the indulgent bosom of her royal husband, remained the confidant of his state secrets, and partook of his kingly beneficence; until at length he had the temerity angrily to expostulate with her, when the indignant sorceress subjected himself and his people to a cruel persecution, from which they were barely rescued by the intervention of a chivalrous and pious sultan.

The Union of North and South had not long existed, ere the former assumed the arrogant airs of Niobe, and proved recreant to her duty, as the lewd wife of the young king of the Black Isles. Those who assert that the *mere* accession of Abraham Lincoln, and his friends, to office and patronage, was the sole cause for the secession of the South, either wilfully pervert the truths of history, or completely fail to comprehend the subject. The success of Mr. Lincoln, as an individual, on the contrary, might have been regarded with indifference; but standing, as he did, upon an aggressive and sectional platform—representing incendiary and revolutionary dogmas of government—and the standard-bearer of an organization, which made war upon property, trampled upon constitutional guarantees, and declared eternal enmity against the social and political institutions of a free and independent people—his elevation to the Presidency of the United States, in defiance of the supplications and protests of almost every mother's child in fifteen sovereign States, was the consummation — the capital crime—and the final victory—of an historical and persistent conspiracy. It was, it is true, the immediate blow which severed the cords of Union; but it was only the ripened fruit of a seed long and widely sown. As early as 1787, the North had a revival of conscience. She made, or thought she had made, the discovery that it was sinful to enslave negroes. But, instead of repenting like a pagan—if not like a Christian—instead of doing penance such as Orestes did—for having sold African slaves to the South, she resolved upon being respectable at the expense of the latter. She caused the Ohio river to be designated as the line which should divide her *Christianity* from the *heathenism* of the South. By virtue of the famous "Missouri Compromise"—that fatally disgraceful, unconstitutional, and un-American measure—this line of demarcation was so amended, as to admit of no slavery, present or prospective, north of latitude 36 degrees and 30 minutes. Step by step, frequently with the "tract oblique" and "indented wave" of the serpent, but latterly with the brazen front of a Corsair, she encroached upon the rights, privileges, and immunities of the South, until at length the dignity and independence of the latter were on the eve of strangulation. The statesmen, political orators, ministers of the Gospel, and representative men in general, of the North, exhausted the vocabulary of misrepresentation, vilification, and insult, assailing and aspersing the South, until, in the frenzy, of vindictive abuse, their mouths became mucilaginous.

Daniel Webster—the most profound of Northern lawyers, but singularly over-estimated as a statesman—wrote in 1850: "From my earliest youth I have regarded slavery as a great moral and political *evil*; and all pretence of defending it on the ground of difference of races, I have ever condemned;"—[because he was either wilfully or invincibly ignorant of the *truth* of both theses.] William H. Seward, in 1858, declared that the institution of slavery promoted "an irrepressible conflict between opposing and enduring forces, which meant that the United States should, sooner or later, become either a slaveholding nation, or entirely a free-labor nation." Salmon P. Chase proposed to "discontinue all action, and repeal all legislation, in favor of slavery at home or abroad, by prohibiting the practice of slaveholding in all places." John C. Fremont—now the American Haynau of Missouri, but in 1856 "Republican" candidate for the Presidency—proclaimed, in accepting of the nomination, that he was "opposed to slavery in the abstract, and upon principles sustained and made habitual by long-settled convictions." Senator Wilson, of Massachusetts, asserted that slavery was "hostile to the rights of human nature," and that there could be no peace between North and South "so long as the foot of an African slave pressed American soil." "We ask," said General Banks in 1856, "that the dead weight of human wrong shall be lifted from the continent again." In the same year, Senator Wade, of Ohio, exclaimed: "there is not a more morbidly suspicious, cruel, revengeful, or lawless despotism, on the face of the earth, than this night-mare of slavery." Joshua R. Giddings, member of Congress from Ohio, prognosticated that "the torch of the incendiary would light up the towns and villages of the South," while the North would "mock at her fears and laugh at her calamities." Anson Burlingame, of Massachusetts, declared in the U. S. House of Representatives, "that slavery had left desolation, ignorance, and death, in its path," and that the North would insist upon having "an anti-slavery Church, an anti-slavery Bible, and an anti-slavery God!" Ralph Waldo Emerson, poet, fanatic, and metaphysician, resolved upon not being outdone as a marvellous slanderer; related to the world how the whip was applied to old men and to tender women—how pregnant women were set in the treadmill for refusing to work—how "men's backs were flayed with cowhides, and hot rum poured on, superinduced with brine and pickle, rubbed in with a corn-husk in the scorching heat of the sun,"—until "the stomach would rise up and curse slavery." * Rev. Theodore Parker assured his hearers, in Music Hall, Boston, that "one day the North would rise in her majesty and put slavery under her feet." Geo. B. Cheever—another pulpitarian—preached that by slavery "the whole family relations, the whole domestic relations, were prostituted, poisoned, and turned into a misery-making machine, for the agent of all evil." Dr. Bellows said : "Our conscientious opposition to slavery is not to be abated or colored by fears of the Union ; and so far as it depends on the North, we are to stop its extension, let the consequences to the Union be what they will." Lewis Tappan was firmly of opinion, that "free christianity recoiled from the leprous touch of slavery." Carl Shurz promulgated that "the despotic power of slavery and mastership combined, pervades the whole political life of the South, like a liquid poison." Wendell Phillips announced, in the hearing of congregated and applauding thousands, in the city of New York, that the pen of the future historian would trace on the blue vault of Heaven, in letters of imperishable immortality, high above the names of Phocion, Fabricius, or Washington, that of the brutal Toussaint L'Ouverture. And the notorious Helper—whose indecently scurrilous book received the warm, and nearly unanimous, endorsement of the great lights of "Republicanism"—published

---

* "Father! forgive the foul calumniator; he knows not what he says."

that it was a " solemn duty to abolish slavery in the South or perish in the attempt ;" that to be a " true patriot one must be an abolitionist ;" that against slaveholders as a body " a war of extermination should be waged, as the time to try the strength of arms and strike the blow had arrived ; that " slaveholders were nuisances and more cruel than murderers," without honor or magnanimity ; that they should be recognized only as ruffians, outlaws, and criminals ; and that the agitation at the North was a " crusade against slavery and the devil."

Thus educated, the North soon learned to spurn the Federal Constitution and the Congressional compromises growing out of it. Her people not only refused to obey, but literally trampled upon the act of Congress, of 1850—better known as the " Fugitive Slave Law :" the Constitution, also, expressly providing that " fugitives from labor " should be restored to their masters, and the Northerners declaring that they should *not*. Indeed, in attempting to carry out the provisions of these sacred enactments, officers of the law were shot down upon the public streets, while endeavoring to discharge their sworn duties ; and the fugitives were rescued from their grasp. When the United States Supreme Court—composed of men endowed with spotless virtue, unsullied integrity, great learning, and purity of character, holding office for life, and removed beyond political influence, or any other future worldly ambition—rendered the celebrated " Dred Scott " decision, establishing that a negro could not become a citizen of the Union, and that the " Missouri Compromise " was unconstitutional ; its exposition of the law was shamefully derided, and the Chief Justice outrageously maligned and denounced for the delivery of such opinion.* The North sent her emissaries to invade, *vi et armis*, the South, and the innocent blood of Virginia's children reddened her soil—her sons were murdered by John Brown and his companions. The property of Southerners was daily stolen or enticed away, and the North rejoiced in the theft and boasted of her cunning and duplicity. She sent her missionaries to the South, with a view of inciting the slaves to effect their escape, by murder, rapine, and insurrection; and some of those

---

* Both in regard to the rendition clause and the status of the territories, the Northern States have assumed to nullify the Constitution. It was with the deliberate purpose of declaring its contempt for the Constitution and for the decrees of the Judges, that the Legislature of the State of New York passed the following concurrent resolution, for which see Laws of 1857 :

STATE OF NEW YORK. }
IN ASSEMBLY, April 16th, 1857. }

Resolved, (If the Senate concur,) That this State will not allow slavery within her borders in any form, or under any pretence, or for any time however short.

Resolved, (If the Senate concur,) That the Supreme Court of the United States, by reason of a majority of the judges thereof having identified with it a sectional and aggressive party, has impaired the confidence and respect of the people of this State.

Resolved, (If the Senate concur,) That the Governor of this State be, and he is hereby respectfully requested, to transmit a copy of these resolutions to the respective Governors of the States of this Union.

By order,

WM. RICHARDSON, Clerk.

IN SENATE, April 18th, 1857.
Passed the Senate.

S. P. ALLEN, Clerk.

It was in urging the passage of these Ordinances of Nullification, that Speaker Littlejohn proclaimed that he "trampled upon the Constitution." It was in reference to this decision that Mr. Seward and his colleagues propose to reörganize the Court by swamping it with a new creation of Abolition Judges. And it was of this decision that Mr. Lincoln spoke, when he said he would not obey it.

philosophically Christian apostles, were detected in the charitable act of poisoning the wells of Texas. Her Representatives in the Federal Congress, employed entire sessions, to the almost total neglect of the general welfare, in the contagious work of agitation; squandering large sums from the public treasury in publishing incendiary documents, and overburdening the mails with reports, furnished by themselves, of their inflammatory speeches. Not a measure, however necessary, even if it were but the building of a new custom house, and intended to benefit the South, could be passed through Congress, without the latter having first agreed to vote millions in lands and moneys, to secure the acquiescence of Western and Northern members. Statesmanship in legislation, or patriotism in parliamentary oratory, entered not into their political ethics. He was, at the North, esteemed the greatest orator, who had best assailed the South, with falsehood, insult, and outrage. He was gloried in as the purest patriot, who had succeeded in legislating away the public lands—in granting bounties from the public treasury to swindling corporations—and in growing independently rich himself, upon a salary of $3,000 a year. Destitute of that Christian spirit of forbearance and moderation, which chastens mankind, and ignoring the code of honor, which renders refined and respectful the intercourse of gentlemen, such legislators used language, so coarse and vile, upon the floors of both houses of Congress, as to recall to the mind of the auditor, the disgraceful scenes in the infamous circus of Byzantium. They respected neither age, talents, nor wisdom. The late venerable Senator Butler, of South Carolina, whose hairs had grown snow-white in the service of his country—who had lived history, and helped to make it—was assailed in the Senate of the United States by Charles Sumner, of Massachusetts, in such vulgar phrase as would bring irrepressible blushes to the cheek of a Billingsgate fish-monger.

And such were the men—such their antecedents, opinions, personal and political characteristics—who assembled in Convention at Chicago, in 1860, to adopt a Confession of Faith, and to put in nomination a candidate for the Presidency—one who was to guide the destinies of over thirty free, independent, sovereign, and Republican States. They adopted a political creed, which was to the Southern States what the Koran of Mohammed was to the unbelieving world—the tocsin of relentless war. This creed "solemnly reässerted the self-evident truths," that the negro was entitled to all the possible or imaginary inalienable rights of the white man; that every inch of the territories of all the States, should be given up to the Northern idea of free institutions; that the Southern institution of servitude should become a sort of prisoner of State, bound by parole of honor, not to obtrude itself outside of certain prescribed limits; and denying to Congress, Territorial Legislatures, or any other earthly powers, the right to introduce slavery beyond such limitations. The next step of this revolutionary conclave was to select a candidate pledged to their views, and Abraham Lincoln was chosen as their representative.

He was an obscure lawyer of the State of Illinois; without a respectable education, or that civil and social culture, which frequently imparts refinement to the conduct of a gentleman, and helps to conceal important defects. Previously to his contest for the Senate, with the late Judge Douglas—a contest which resulted in his defeat—he was comparatively unknown. His knowledge of Government and affairs of State, were confined to his practice as attorney in County and State Courts; and his political experience, to the Western stump and the village bar-room. But his opinions were known—opinions of which he seems to have been as vain as Goldsmith's pedagogue was of his own acquirements—and they tallied with those of the Chicago Junta. As we have illustrated and established, the negro is an inferior being. Before he becomes our equal he must be recreated—the God of Nature and of peoples must recast him in another and finer mould—his whole frame will have to undergo regeneration from degradation of type—his intellect must be burnished with superior inspiration— and his superficial form assume an æsthetic aspect. But of what avail could these truths be to the understanding of Mr. Lincoln, who, in the sphere of reason, never rose to the dignity of Blaise Pascal's "thinking reed?" Blind to the immutable facts of science and philosophy, he would have the negro the equal of Washington and Cincinnatus—of Socrates and Cato! In 1856, he declared that mankind were marching in "steady progress toward equality for all men." Two years later, he advised his friends to "discard all things and unite as one people throughout the land, until they should once more stand up declaring that all men were created equal." In the same year, he said: "I do assert now, however, so there need be no difficulty about it, that I desire slavery should be put in a course of ultimate extinction. * * I have always hated slavery, I think, as much as any abolitionist. * * 'A house divided against itself cannot stand.' I believe that this Government cannot endure permamently half slave and half free. * * I do not expect the house to fall, but I do expect it will cease to be divided: it will become one thing, or all the other. Either the opponents of slavery will arrest the further spread of it, and place it where the public mind shall rest in the belief that it is in the course of ultimate extinction, or its advocates will push it forward till it shall become alike lawful in all the States, old as well as new, North as well as South." And again: "If I were in Congress, and a vote should come up on a question whether slavery should be prohibited in a new Territory, in spite of the Dred Scott decision, [no matter as to his oath,] I would vote that it should." Firm, then, in this the faith of his party, and boldly expressing such opinions, he received the "Republican" nomination—accepted it—pledged himself to the maintenance of the agrarian principles of the Chicago platform—and was elected President.

There were those at the South, who, wearied of the long and persistent strife—wearied of the repeated inroads made upon their rights—wearied of expostulating with men who insulted alike their patient sufferings and their warnings—regarded with indifference, if not with joy, the headlong frenzy of the people of the North: for in the triumph of Lincoln, they beheld the deliverance of the South. But there were statesmen there also, who were devoted in their attachment to the union of the States, and to the Constitution which was their bond of partnership—men of exalted patriotism, gifted with powers of oratory and persuasion, and backed by the great conservative elements of their section. They were sent as commissioned delegates, during the Presidential canvass, with words of love and sorrow, to remonstrate with the fanatics of the North—to

9

supplicate them not to destroy the Union.   But their mission met with derision.   Their speeches were received with something like idiotic mirth, or responded to with shouts of maniacal defiance.   They were told that the South could not be kicked out of the Union—that her threats were mere bluster—that the chivalry of her sons resembled the courage of Bob Acres.   They were told, in addition, that if the South were out of the Union, she could not be induced to remain so long.   They were gravely informed that out of the Union the South would starve; that she could not raise sufficient provisions to feed her slaves; that without Northern hay her cattle would perish;* that without Northern manufacturers,

---

* It is is not much to the credit of the intelligence of the Northern masses, to relate that such convictions obtained almost universality amongst them.   They were indoctrinated to so believe by false teachers.   Their error is well exposed in the following comparison of Southern and Northern productive resources, taken from the Mobile *Advertiser:*

"We will select, first, South Carolina to run the parallel with, for several reasons, the chief of which are, that she has been supposed to produce nothing but cotton and rice, and she is the most derided and contemned of all the slaveholding States.   Not many persons are aware that this State alone produces five-sixths nearly of all the rice grown, but the Seventh Census, of 1850, shows that to be the fact; besides nearly all the rice, she produces wheat to within 3,000 bushels of all produced by the six New England States together.   She produces almost as much corn as the State of New York, and 6,000,000 of bushels of that grain more than all the New England States together, for she produced upwards of 16,000,000 bushels.   She produces more oats than Maine; more by 1,000,000 of bushels than Massachusetts; more than 1,000,000 bushels of potatoes over and above what Maine produced; more beans and peas by 180,000 bushels than all the Northern States together, except New York; more beef cattle than Pennsylvania by 1,740, and almost as many as all the New England States together; more sheep than Iowa and Wisconsin by 10,699; more hogs than New York by 47,251, more than Pennsylvania by

her people would become semi-naked and semi-barbarous;

25,137, and 86,000 more than all the New England States, with New Jersey, Michigan, Wisconsin, and California in the bargain; more horses and mules by 10,000 than Maine, New Hampshire, Massachusetts, and Rhode Island together; besides all which she produces largely of oxen, cows, and a variety of products of the smaller kinds.

"Virginia and North Carolina produced jointly 13,363,000 bushels of wheat, or 241,000 more than the great wheat State of New York, or a quantity equal to the whole product of the six New England States, with New Jersey, Michigan, Iowa and Wisconsin, all put together. Virginia, North Carolina and Tennessee produced 115,471,593 bushels of corn, a quantity exceeding by 300,000 bushels the joint product of New York, Pennsylvania, Ohio, New Jersey, Connecticut, New Hampshire, Vermont and Maine.

"Tennessee alone produces 16,500 more hogs than all the six New England States, with New York, Pennsylvania, New Jersey, Iowa and Michigan; for that State produced 3,104,800 hogs, while the eleven Northern States named produced but 3,088,394. Most people have thought that the North was really the hog-producing section, but such is by no means the fact; the whole number of hogs produced in 1850 was 30,316,608, of which the slaveholding States furnished 20,770,730, or more than two-thirds of the whole swine production.

"It will doubtless surprise many persons to be told that the seven Gulf or Cotton States of South Carolina, Georgia, Alabama, Mississippi, Louisiana, Arkansas and Texas, produce 45,187 more beef than the six New England States, New York, Pennsylvania, Ohio, New Jersey, Indiana, Michigan and Wisconsin altogether; but such is the fact, for the census of 1850 tells us these seven Cotton States produced 3,357,489 beef cattle, while the thirteen Northern States named produced 3,312,237.

"A single glance at the live stock columns of the Seventh Census will prove to the inquirer that the slaveholding States produced more beef-cattle than the non-slaveholding by 1,782,587. That while the North produced 2,541,121 cows, the South produced 3,829,810. That the Northern States produced 866,396 work-oxen against 820,340 produced by the Southern States. That while the North produced 2,310,961 horses and mules, the South produced 250,358 more, for the Southern production was 2,570,319."

that but for Northern protection, she would be crushed
beneath the angry heel of servile insurrection; in short,
that she was neither useful nor ornamental to the North,
only as a mere appanage of empire.

O, Jerusalem! Jerusalem! that stonest the prophets
and slayest those that are sent unto thee! The North
spurned the counsels of the patriotic and the wise—followed the leadership of demagogues, fanatics, and false
teachers—and on the 6th day of November, 1860, played
the last act in a Nation's tragedy; deliberately
walked up to the ballot-box; elected Abraham Lincoln;
*solemnly violated her part of the Federal contract; and
severed forever the sacred cords of Union and fraternity between the States.* SHE WAS THE ORIGINAL AND
WILFUL SECESSIONIST. But South Carolina responded
next day: RESURGAM! The following month found
her out of the Union. The Revolution spread "with
giant beard of flame." Mississippi, Texas, Florida,
Georgia, Alabama, and Louisiana, soon followed her example. The work of ruin commenced at the North.
Mercantile houses failed to meet the demands of their
creditors; banks suspended specie payments; mechanics
and laborers were suddenly cast out of employment; im-
portations from foreign countries ceased, and ships lay
idle in their docks. The prophets who heralded the
advent of Mr. Lincoln, had previously inoculated the
North with the conviction, that his elevation to the Presidency would quiet agitation—would put an end to discord—would usher in the golden days of peace, harmony,
and prosperity: hence all eyes were turned to him for
relief. He was implored by suffering millions to come
forward and stem the torrent—to allay the fears of men
—to give assurances of justice, equality, and protection

in their rights, to the disaffected; but his lips were closed by other hands; the prayers of his petitioners, were treated by him with much of that mute stolidity, stripped however of the venerable dignity which adds mystery to the silence, of the Sphynx of Cheops. *Salutare tuum exspectabo, Domine,* was the sublime exclamation of the pious Jacob; and with kindred resignation, the North now waited for the hour when the opening of her oracle's lips would impart balm to the nation's heart.

At length the hegira from Illinois to Washington commenced; and Mr. Lincoln, at the moment when the whole country was in revolutionary chaos, informed starving women and idle men, that "nobody was hurt." For the first time the film was momentarily removed from the eyes of the North. Her people apprehended that the power of their ruler was founded upon their own folly; and that his fancied greatness rested upon a basis of weakness.

Contrition generally follows the commission of a wrong act, and they were seemingly contrite—feignedly, but boisterously so. The heart-desolation of our first parents, upon their expulsion from Paradise—the affliction of Job—the regret of Jonas in the bowels of the whale —or the grief of that father whose son was sold into Egyptian bondage—could not compare with the bitter sorrow of the North, upon her awaking to a full realization of her sin. But progression, not retrogression, is the distinguishing quality of vice. As the spider weaves the fly into the labyrinth of his web, so the fanaticism of a people envelopes a State in ruin; and this repentance of the North, being brief and evanescent, she had not the moral qualities of redeeming her errors, by attempting to repair the injuries which she had inflicted, for she never recognized a nice distinction in either ethics or politics.

Her Congress was in session; she had laid upon its tables numerous petitions, praying that *something* might be done to heal the wound and restore health to the body politic. But her Representatives were composed of knaves and fools, possessed of the twin disease of ignorance and dishonesty. They spurned alike prayers and arguments; they exulted in the banishment of patriots and statesmen from the halls of legislation; and they finally converted the last Congress of the United States into a hospital for revolutionists, office-seekers, and speculators. Every measure of peace and conciliation proposed in that body, and designed to secure the permanent autonomy of the Republic, came from the South. Amongst numerous others, Senator Toombs, of Georgia, brought forward a plan of reconciliation, in harmony with the Constitution, and the principles upon which the Federation was founded, but it was disdainfully rejected. Senator Crittenden, of Kentucky, came forth with proposed amendments to the Constitution. Their provisions were humiliating to the South, un-American in spirit, and, like all compromises, calculated to inspire future agitation; yet, with the hope of avoiding *immediate* disunion and civil war, the Representatives of the South voted for their adoption; but they were contemptuously defeated by those of the North. Senator Davis, of Mississippi—now the patriot President of the Confederate States—introduced a series of resolutions infringing upon no right of the North, and only securing to the South, that which the Constitution and the laws, as expounded by the Supreme Court, declared to be her just dues; but they were scornfully voted down. The great, ancient and dignified State of Virginia—the mother of sages, statesmen, and heroes, in whose soil repose the remains of Washington, Jefferson, and Madison—proposed the holding of a "Peace Convention," where all the States might be represented, with a determination of adjusting existing difficulties, and of restoring harmony once more to the distracted Union. The Convention met. It was composed of many eminent men, of exalted station, wise in years, and, like Pylian Nestor, sage in council. A majority of all the States were represented there. After long and wearied deliberations, extending over whole weeks, and while a nation's anxious eyes, hopeful and expectant, were rivetted upon them, they agreed upon a political catholicon—one-sided, as usual, and unjust to the South. It was submitted to Congress, now a Republican rump and cabal; but it failed to meet, on the part of the North, with either decent or respectful consideration. Every plea for conciliation—every measure for concession proposed—were treated by these madmen, as so many evidences of "rebel" weakness and vacillation. The temple of their liberties was on fire, but instead of water, they cast oil upon the flames.

Concession might have disarmed prejudice; might have restored health to discontent; would certainly have arrested the progress of revolution. But "Republican" Senators and Members of Congress were adverse to so wise a policy. Minerva had forsaken them. They clung to a vulgar policy of "consistency" in error; forgetting that true statesmanship does not depend upon servile subserviency to past fallacies of opinion. The truly consistent statesman, will not so much consider his mistakes in the past, as he will what it is his duty to accomplish for the present and the future. The late

Sir Robert Peel once overthrew a British administration, and rode into power upon the hobby of "protection;" but in a few years later, the fallacy of his policy became to him self-evident, and he did not hesitate to swallow his own political sword. Both he and the Duke of Wellington had previously performed a similar feat of deglutition, when they conceded Catholic emancipation to Ireland. And a greater than either of them—a greater, in political wisdom, than any Briton that ever lived (Bacon excepted)—Edmund Burke—when he found that the interests of a whole empire demanded it, ignored, and set at defiance, the commands of his constituents. But the representative men of the North were not to be governed by the dictates of a universal policy. Creatures of narrow minds and easy virtue, they were ruled by passion and corruption in their actions. They assailed with crimination and threats, those whom they had grossly wronged and injured, and recrimination and defiance were flouted back into their teeth. They persevered in malignity, until the affections of those whom benevolence rendered kindly disposed to them, were alienated from their section and their Government.

At length the 4th day of March, 1861, arrived. It was the day upon which Abraham Lincoln was to be inaugurated President. A rival Government—the future hope of the Southern Republic—was established and in full force, at Montgomery, Alabama. It had possession of nearly all the arsenals and fortifications in seven sovereign States, whose people were pledged to maintain their inalienable freedom and independence. Forts Sumter and Pickens were beleaguered with armed and resolute men. All hopes of peace, amity, and fraternity,

depended upon the policy of Mr. Lincoln. The hour
for his inauguration came. He was surrounded by all
the pomp and circumstances of solemnity. The oath,
to support the laws and carry out in their integrity the
provisions of the Constitution, was to be administered
to him by the Chief Justice of that Court, whose high
behests he had previously boasted that he would not
obey, when contrary to his preconceived notions. From
the hand of that venerable functionary, however, he
received the sacred book of God's written laws; after
his lips he repeated the words which sealed a bond
betwixt him and Heaven. How he has respected this
awful bond, chaining him to the responsibility of the
hereafter of life—how he has violated the Constitution
and the laws—how he has trampled upon human
liberty—how he has made war without authority—how
he has strangled the press—how he has wantonly destroyed public property—and how he has set an example
to mankind, of immorality, perjury, and godlessness, we
will presently have to relate.

But the next scene of the mournful drama was the
reading of the inaugural. It matters not whether this
address was, or was not, written by Mr. Seward; the
Northern President is responsible for it. Its words
were as skillfully ambiguous as those of a Delphic
Oracle. Like the veil of Mokanna, it was made the
instrument of concealing dark designs, iniquitous and
flagitious. Senators from Delaware, Maryland, Virginia,
Kentucky, Arkansas, Missouri, and North Carolina, remained after the adjournment of Congress, in an extra
session of the Senate, to confirm Executive appoint-
ments and transact other public business. Daily they
beheld the future policy of the new President fore-

shadowed. He nominated as his staff, to every depart-
ment of the public service, notorious abolitionists and
unrelenting coercionists. He made William H. Seward
Secretary of State; Salmon P. Chase Secretary of the
Treasury; and Montgomery Blair Postmaster General.
He sent Anson Burlingame as his representative to
Austria; Cassius M. Clay to Russia; Carl Schurz to
Spain; Jas. E. Harvey to Portugal; Charles F. Adams
to England; and Joshua R. Giddings to Canada. Thus,
the statesman of the South, who remained in the old
Senate Chamber, witnessed the subversion of the principles which had long imparted prosperity and stability
to the American Government. They beheld rank revolutionists and incendiary politicians, pledged to the overthrow of their dearest institutions, seize the reins of
power. But accustomed to obey the laws, they acquiesced, and confirmed the nominations of Mr. Lincoln.
And the hour for concession having passed, the intervals
of the session not occupied by the transactions of Executive business, were improved by them in endeavoring to
learn from their Republican colleagues, what policy the
Government would pursue toward the Confederate States.
They knew that a restoration or reconstruction of the
Union had become impracticable; but before the curtain
was drawn over the last Congress of the United States,
it was their wish to leave to the people a legacy of peace.
In speeches, infused with eloquence and fraught with the
essence of purest patriotism, they addressed themselves
to those who now wielded power, either for good or
evil. They counselled moderation, conciliation, amity.
But they were laconically told that "the laws would be
enforced." Those who never obeyed the laws, or revered
the Federal Constitution—who made it their jocund boast

to have violated each—and who were soon to trample upon every vestige of State and individual rights—now affected supreme love for both. They were conspiring to "let slip the dogs of war." Soon the din of arms was to resound along the line of border States; along the Mississippi and the Potomac; brother would meet brother in the shock of death; a war would be waged, which would make Hell rejoice—a war of subjugation and extermination, waged by the North against the South.

XVI.

A GOVERNMENT which does not rest upon the consent of the governed, is necessarily an odious and bad government—bad, because even the benefits it may confer are the fruits of usurpation. If the axiom be true, that the power of governing is but the commission of God to the ruler, the trust is sufficiently onerous and responsible, even when willingly acquiesced in by the governed. But for him that usurps power to rule over a people who despise him, there can be no other name than TYRANT. To govern a people against their will, is a crime against humanity, an insult to reason, and an outrage upon liberty. Such a ruler must, of necessity, be a conqueror. His jurisdiction is maintained by the remorseless ravage of States—by covering his path with death, terror, and desolation—by rendering himself hateful to the virtuous; sacrificing the heroic, and enslaving the free. The bravest of his friends and foes fall together, the victims of his pride, tyranny, and usurpation. Hav-

ing become himself the first violator of public law, his
followers will emulate his evil example, until general
crime takes the place of regular order, and the fiercer
passions of hatred and revenge, substitute humanity and
sociology. By his influence, commerce and agriculture
are ruined—the plastic and mechanic arts sink into decrepitude—science, literature, and religion are neglected
or forgotten—demoralization becomes contagious—good
men are forced, or deluded, into a co-partnership of
action with the despicable—villainy and profligacy are
licensed to invade the sanctuaries of virtue and purity—
and while innocence and industry are stripped of armor
and shield, indecency and crime stalk abroad gigantic,
unchecked, and unpunished: for these are inevitable
consequences of war.

And even when war is justly waged; when it is fortified by principles of humanity and right; when the
patriot's sword is unsheathed to defend his country's
liberties; its evils are only extenuated, but not obliterated. It brings jealousy and rivalry into the camp of
friends; it covers the earth with carnage; it strips the
parent of the child; it divorces the husband from his
wife; it sets villages and cities in flames; it converts
happy homes into temples of misery and mourning; it
makes of smiling Ceres a woful Suppliant; and the
proudest victory is achieved upon the ruins of a flourish-
ing glory. The martyr's crown, and the praise of history, may reward the patriot who falls in defence of his
freedom; but when the sword is drawn to oppress, he
who wields it is a murderer and a robber.

But since the world began—since war first cursed
earth and degraded man—it would be difficult to discover, in the pages of universal history, the record of

so unholy and iniquitous a civil strife, as that into which Abraham Lincoln has plunged the American States. The war which he wages is a bastard begotten of power and arrogance. He, his advisers, and the section of the old Republic to which he belongs, had, during the quarter of a century previous to his inauguration, heaped abuse, and outrage, and wrong, upon the people they are now endeavoring to crush, subjugate, and exterminate. They represented that the South hung, like a mill-stone, round the neck of the Union, retarding her progress and blighting her prosperity. They inculcated in all of their moral teachings and political proclamations — some directly and others indirectly — that she would be "let slide," or that slavery should be abolished, ere the North could take her proper place among the nations. And, resolved at length to preserve her institutions, protect her property, and bear the responsibility of her own sins and disadvantages, the South separated herself from what seemed to be a dissatisfied partner; but implored a continuance of peace and friendship in parting. Here the North changed front. She declared that the South should not depart; that she should still remain in the Union, but as an inferior, without the protection guarantied by the Constitution, and stripped of her four thousand millions of dollars' worth of slave property.

This is not the language of exaggeration; it is the doctrine promulgated by the Northern press, enunciated by Northern leaders, and practiced and carried out by Northern generals, ever since the godless invasion of the Northern hordes begun. Charles Sumner, in a speech recently delivered by him before the Republican Convention of the State of Massachusetts, declared that slavery should be abolished, and the South conquered. Wendell Phillips, the Belial of this great infernal plot, whose

"——————— ———————— tongue
Dropp'd manna, and could make the worse appear
The better reason, "

in language more classical and forcible than that of his rhetorical colleague in crime, maintained that such was the object of this relentless war. Gen. Jim Lane said there would be an army of *one color* marching into Slave States, and an army of *another color* marching out. Rev. Dr. Bellows, in consecrating the arms of Northern regiments, invoked God to speed the abolition cause. Rev. Dr. R. J. Breckinridge declared that this rebellion shall be put down, it matters not at what expenditure of money, or what sacrifice of the blood of rebels, or their wives and children! The Rev. Dr. Hitchcock, the Rev. Mr. Goodell, John Jay, Oliver Johnson, and other shining lights of the North, lay and clerical, have gone still farther than Phillips or Sumner. At a public meeting held a few weeks since in the city of New York, convened for the purpose of devising a plan whereby the present fratricidal conflict should be made "short and decisive," it was resolved that "the speedy and complete liberation of the slaves on the soil," had become a necessity; that to effect this, "the free colored people of the United States should be encouraged to enlist in the great enterprise;" and that, as Leo X. had said, not only the Christian religion, but Nature, cried out against slavery. "The utmost good nature pervaded the meeting, and the feeling in favor of the *immediate abolition of slavery,* as a necessity of the war power, was unanimous," according to the *New York Times.* This same journal afterwards inculcated, that there could be no peace—no end of war—no compromise—while slavery existed. The *Chicago Tribune*—understood to be the leading organ of Mr. Lincoln in Illinois—re-echoed the language of the *Times*, branded the Southern institution as the sum of all villainies, and laid down the axiom, that "whenever a slave is claimed as the property of another, the claimant is a traitor and a rebel." "In the course of events," says the *Boston Transcript*, "the hour has arrived for settling the question, whether the inherent despotism of the slave power, or a republic true to freedom, shall rule from the lakes to the gulf, from ocean to ocean." "We hold that slavery is the cause of the war," responds the Delaware (N. Y.) *Express*, "and that it is the duty of those in whom lie the power, to rid the country of this cause." "The North is in arms against slavery," exclaims the Rockland (Me.) *Gazette;* "it is fighting against the slavery interest and nothing else." "There cannot and never will be peace again in what formed the United States, so long as slavery exists in the South," is an apothegm from the Harrisburg (Pa.) *Telegraph*. The New York *World* will accept from the South not even "abdication." "When there is danger," it adds, "that it shall come to that, let slaveholders beware. The day it is settled that either slavery or the government must perish, that day slavery will be doomed." And again : "If the North cannot conquer rebellion without emancipation, it will conquer it with emancipation." "Close the column and let the battle rage with Napoleonic fury; while the earth shall open to receive, heaven will expand to accommodate the spirits of those that shall fall"—shouts the Cincinnati *Times*, borrowing its theology from Mohammed.

In harmony with this settled purpose — with such devilish and fanatical teachings — and with the long nurtured resolution of their section, the Northern army and its officers, immediately upon their invasion of Southern soil, commenced a remorseless pillage of slave property. This policy was a part of the war strategy of General Rosencranz in Western Virginia — a policy whereby it was hoped to make wavering minds loyal to the "Union." It was practised by Gen. B. F. Butler, while he commanded at Fortress Monroe, upon a splendid scale; his hired myrmidons having robbed farmers, whose only crime was devotion to freedom, of over one thousand negroes—which the invaders naively denominated "contrabands." And this exploit of degraded rapine, on the part of an inglorious and pusillanimous commander, was sanctioned by President Lincoln's Secretary of War, Simon Cameron. But it was reserved for Gen. Fremont to cross the Rubicon of Barbarism — to endeavor to have re-enacted, in the South, that ineffably horrible spectacle which desecrated the soil of Hayti. Appointed major-general to command the Federal army in, and subjugate the State of Missouri, one of his first official acts was to issue an edict of emancipation to the blacks! Regarding this step as politically imprudent and premature, until his heel could be more firmly planted upon the necks of Maryland and Kentucky, Mr. Lincoln requested his subordinate to "modify" the proclamation. But Fremont knew his master's heart. He disregarded the request, had a new supply printed after its receipt, and circulated his own decree broad-cast over Missouri.

There is an identity in the acts of tyrants, which cannot fail of making sad impressions upon the mind of a historian. Twice, within a period of less than a single century, have two different and implacable foes sought the bloody spoliation of the South, by means of servile insurrections. On the 7th day of November, 1775, Lord Dunmore issued, in Virginia, a proclamation similar in spirit and intent to that addressed by Gen. Fremont, in 1861, to the people of Missouri. "You may observe," writes the former three days afterwards to General Howe, "that I offer freedom to the blacks of all white rebels that join me, in consequence of which there are two or three hundred already come in, and those I form into corps as fast as they come in, giving them white officers and non-commissioned in proportion. And from this plan I make no doubt of getting men enough *to reduce this colony to a proper sense of their duty.*" A Virginia Convention indignantly responded to the proclamation; but the final reply was given by George Washington, at the cannon's mouth, before Yorktown, to Lord Cornwallis, in 1781. And how well Missouri has emulated these noble examples, in answering the ordinance of Fremont, let the battles which she fought, and the victories which she won, at Springfield and Lexington, relate: for there is a coincidence of virtue in the deeds of patriots, as there is of baseness in the actions of tyrants.

But it is melancholy, because it is far from being hopeful to the cause of human freedom, to reflect that from the great experiment of American liberty, could spring a government, characterized by a despotic frenzy, which overshadows that of the administration of Lord North: and that, more than a century ago, the relations of master and servant should have been better understood by an Irishman, than they are now by our adver-

10

saries. "The high aristocratic spirit of Virginia and the Southern Colonies, it has been proposed, I know," said Edmund Burke, "to reduce, by declaring a general enfranchisement of their slaves. This project has had its advocates and panegyrists; yet I never could argue myself into any opinion of it. Slaves are often much attached to their masters. A general wild offer of liberty would not always be accepted. History furnishes few instances of it. It is sometimes as hard to persuade slaves to be free, as it is to compel freemen to be slaves. * * * But when we talk of enfranchisement, do we not perceive that the American master may enfranchise too, and arm servile hands in defence of freedom? * * * Slaves, as these black people are, and dull as all people are from slavery, must they not a little suspect the offer of freedom from *that very nation which has sold them to their present masters?*" But Burke, who looked over the heads of centuries, spoke truth in vain. George III. and Lord North resolved upon the subjugation of the colonists. The colonists were British subjects—they were children of Great Britain—they owed allegiance to the English crown—they were "rebels"—the British Constitution was founded upon justice and benignity, and its supremacy should be maintained; albeit Americans were deprived of a full participation in its benefits.

The fruit of this insolently wicked policy has passed into the morals of history. And yet it is revived, copied, adopted, by the administration of Abraham Lincoln. They have both perverted and violated the Constitution of their country. That grand instrument of human liberty, begotten of the wisdom of purest statesmanship, baptized in the blood of noblest patriots, and fostered through a long term of suffering and self-denial, has been by them corrupted and defloured. According to its own preamble, it was framed to "establish justice, ensure domestic tranquility, provide for the common defence, and promote the general welfare" of the several States embraced in the perfect Union. But according to Mr. Lincoln and his Cabinet, its purpose was to consummate a consolidated nationality, and overthrow the integrity of State sovereignty. "The powers not delegated to the United States by the Constitution"—reads the tenth article of the great Charter—"are reserved to *the States respectively*, or to the people." "The States have no power, other than that which they derive from the *Nation*," replies the Government at Washington.

But the States were separate, sovereign, and independent, before the Constitution had existence. They were sovereign, independent, and separate, when they rebelled against the despotic authority of the mother country. Governor Bernard, in his official dispatches, styled them "the American Governments." And they remained, respectively, independent, separate, and sovereign, *after* the Constitution was ordained. Some of these *governments* refused, for a time, to adopt it as a league of alliance. Even when they acceded, they still retained their individual constitutions, legislatures, laws, distinctive usages, and every paraphernalia of freedom; and where usurpation (as in Maryland) has not prevailed, they do so now. The Federal Constitution had to be ratified by the Conventions of the respective States: by this mode only it could attain the virtue of becoming vital. Had it been rejected by a majority of the States, it would have forever remained inanimate. But having been adopted—did it necessarily follow that in the case of its violation, it must be perpetual—that it was to remain binding forever upon the unborn generations of the incomprehensible future? If so, then it resembles wedlock, which none but God should put asunder. If so, it is an anomaly in legislation; or, all legislative acts are irrepealable and eternal. "But here is an extraordinary case—a case of public polity," objects the sophist. Aye, but it is, nevertheless, a mere matter of international contract; and Equity, the handmaiden of Justice, must rule States by the same standard which is prescribed to individuals. "A bargain broken on one side is broken on both," said Daniel Webster—in discussing a similar topic—than whom, whatever may have been his defects as a statesman, there was no greater expositor of the Constitution and the laws.

But, in the expression of this opinion, he simply co-incided with the well known doctrines of the Revolutionary fathers. *They* never regarded the Union other than a confederacy of States, leagued together "for the common defence, and to promote the general welfare." And so the several Governments viewed it; otherwise the Union never would have been formed. Mr. Madison maintained that a breach of the fundamental principles of Union compact, by any one part of the societies composing it, would fully absolve the other parts from their voluntary obligations to it; because that the Federal Union constituted a mere convention of individual States, governed by the law of nations, from which it resulted, that "a breach of any one article, by any one party, left all the other parties at liberty to consider the convention as dissolved." From the earliest *thought* of Union, until the illicit introduction of modern heresy, this was the political philosophy of American Government. "Each State retains its sovereignty, freedom and independence, and every power, jurisdiction, and right, which is not by this Confederation expressly delegated to the United States"—reads the second of the articles of the old Confederation. "The said States," says the next article, "hereby severally enter into a firm *league of* FRIENDSHIP with each other, for their common defence, the securities of their Liberties, and their mutual and general welfare, binding themselves *to assist each other.*" Here is the testimony of the Dead, vindicating the original and invariable attitude of the South, and illustrating the doctrines which created the old Union. And when these articles proved inadequate— when it became necessary that Congress should have the power of raising a revenue to sustain Government and pay off the Revolutionary debt—and when, accordingly, the present Federal Constitution was framed, the States, with singular caution and jealousy, watched and guarded the securities of their individual sovereignties. For commercial reasons, the State of Rhode Island refused to adopt the Constitution, until two years had transpired after its adoption by eleven of the other States. North Carolina remained, for other reasons, but similar in principle, one year out of the Union. And Maryland remained three years out of the old Confederation, because the extent of Virginia's share of the territories was so great as to endanger the future equilibrium of State sovereignty. Virginia at length magnanimously removed this cause of difficulty, by ceding her western territorial empire to the Convention of States; out of which gift have since been formed, the great and antagonistic Commonwealths of Ohio, Indiana, Illinois, and Michigan. So Achilles lent his arms to

Patroclus, not indeed to be used against him or the Hellenic cause; but Hector, in the armor of Pelides, could not be deemed more unnatural by Hellas, than to the eye of reason, appears the strange sight of these States, arming to subjugate their parental benefactress, and suffocate the principles which gave them liberty and life.

But in the face of this attempted matricidal crime— this sin of black ingratitude—and of a devastating invasion—in defiance of the fundamental tenets of the Revolution, and of the time-hallowed doctrines of the Fathers, those States are now in arms against nature, history, and reason. As early as 1798, the author of the Declaration of Independence, Mr. Jefferson, held "that the several States composing the United States of America, are not united on the principle of unlimited submission to their General Government; but that * * * as in all other cases of compact, having no common judge, each party has an equal right to judge for itself, as well of infractions as of the mode and measure of redress." And this was the theory espoused by Patrick Henry, James Madison, Edmund Randolph, Mason and Nicholas. The idea of the General Government's having any power other than that of mere agency, was regarded as un-American and iniquitous. " To coerce the States is one of the maddest projects that was ever devised," said Alexander Hamilton. "This Constitution," asserted Mr. Ellsworth, does not attempt to coerce sovereign bodies, States, in their political capacities. No coercion is applicable to such bodies." And during the seventy-two years of our past American self-government, the Constitution was administered sixty of those years, in harmony with these Southern principles, and mainly

by Southern statesmen. Washington's rule lasted eight
years; Jefferson, Madison, and Monroe, ruled twenty-
four years; Jackson was President eight years; and the
reins of Government were wielded for sixteen years by
Harrison, Tyler, Polk, Taylor, Fillmore, and Pierce.
Add to these, the four years' administration of President
Buchanan, and we have sixty, out of the seventy-two
years, of Southern policy in increasing the grandeur
and perpetuating the liberty of America. But throughout this period it was never denied, to any considerable
or dangerous extent, that the people of one generation,
and of any one political Commonwealth, had the right
to duly assemble in Convention, and alter or modify
their present institutions. The sovereignty of the
States was conceded to be the sheet-anchor of the
Republic—was regarded as sacred, inherent, inalienable,
and unrestricted. For instance (and merely as an illustration), in the year 1845, it was proposed to admit
Texas as a State into the league of United States.
On the 1st day of March, by joint resolution, Congress
consented "that the territory properly included and
rightfully belonging to *the Republic of Texas* may be
erected into a new State;" and that "the said Republic
of Texas *shall retain* all the public funds, debts, taxes,
and dues of every kind, which may belong to or be due
and owing said Republic," &c. &c.; "*but in no event are
said debts and liabilities to become a charge on the
Government of the United States.*" Here we witness
the latter power in the character of an agent, but the
former in the garments of a sovereign. On the 29th
day of December following, it was declared by Congress,
"That the State of Texas shall be one, and is hereby
declared to be one, of the United States of America, and

admitted into the Union on an equal footing with the
original States." That "footing" consisted of being
secured in the guarantees of the Federal Constitution,
which stipulates upon its face, to insure every State a
republican form of government, and their people, to the
latest posterity, the blessings of liberty.

Now this was a contract, with well-marked and carefully defined limits, between the United States of
America and the Republic of Texas, resembling, in a
moral sense at least, every other honorable covenant
made between men or nations; and the latter, finding
the conditions of the league violated—finding usurpation
instead of Republicanism—tyranny in lieu of liberty—
war in the place of blessings—injustice for equity—
would she not, of natural right, be absolved from the
partnership, and have "an equal right to judge for herself as well of infractions as of the mode and measure
of redress?" He who would deny it, has studied
neither Grotius nor Vattel—Blackstone nor Kent—
he is ignorant of law.

This, however, is not fable; it is fact. The principles
upon which rested the edifice of Union have been ruthlessly subverted. The sovereignty of the States has
not only been invaded, but its existence pronounced a
mere myth. State Conventions have been dispersed;
State Legislatures banished or imprisoned; State laws
set at open defiance; State elections tampered with and
corrupted; and the United States gazetted to mankind
as a CONSOLIDATED NATIONALITY. "The Union gave
each of the States"—wrote Mr. Lincoln in his Message
to the Northern Congress, July, 1861—" whatever independence and liberty it had. The Union is older than

any of the States, and in fact it created them as States."*
The brazen effrontery of these falsehoods, or the invincible ignorance of their author, might well excite either the pity or contempt of a philosopher, did not history teach that audacity and perfidy are characteristics of tyrants. The Commonwealth of Virginia, whose sages were instrumental in forming the Union, and out of whose territories were made sovereign States, is told that she is younger than the Union; North Carolina, which hesitated for more than one year to ratify the Constitution of the United States, is taught that by the Union she was first made a State; and the Republic of Texas is informed, that "whatever independence or liberty she had," flowed from the same source! Surely the North has a Daniel in her Presidential chair.

"I do solemnly swear, that I will faithfully execute the office of President of the United States, and will, to the best of my ability, *preserve*, protect, and defend, the Constitution of the United States "—was the inau-

---

*Such is his opinion. But in a speech delivered by him, in the United States House of Representatives, January 12th, 1848, he said: "Any people, anywhere, being inclined, and having the power, have the right to rise up and shake off the existing government, and form a new one that suits them better. This is a most valuable, a most sacred right—a right which we hope and believe is to liberate the world. Nor is the right confined to cases in which the whole people of an existing government may choose to exercise it. Any portion of such people that *can*, *may* revolutionize, and make their own of so much of the territory as they inhabit. More than this, a majority of any portion of such people may revolutionize, putting down a minority intermingled with, or near about them, who may oppose their movements. Such minority was precisely the case of the tories of our own revolution. It is a quality of revolutions not to go by *old* LINES, or *old laws;* but to break up both, and make *new ones.*"

guration oath of Abraham Lincoln. That Constitution recognizes the sovereign independence of each and every State—guarantees to them separate and free forms of government—renders their laws and possessions exempt from all external influences—upholds them as equal partners of a general agency—gave to Congress the power of *regulating* the territories for the mutual advantage of all—and clothed it with absolute and exclusive jurisdiction (except in adjusting what might promote the general welfare), only in a district of ten miles square: but Mr. Lincoln interpreted the Constitution, and respected his oath, so as to render State Governments mere nullities—political toys—non-entities. He created new offices, and swarmed upon independent States hireling myrmidons to devour their substance. He raised standing armies without law and without authority. He rendered the military power absolute over the civil. And he made the jurisdiction of the Constitution the slave of his will. The right of the Federal authority to make war upon, or coerce a State into obedience, was, in the Convention that framed it, indignantly denied to the Constitution; but he has 'undertaken to subjugate and lay waste fourteen States, and to crush their peoples beneath the fiery heel of war. Congress alone had power to raise and support armies; and to provide for organizing and disciplining the militia; but he usurped this power by issuing his proclamation calling 75,000 men into the field. Congress alone had the right to declare war, to provide for and maintain a navy; but this power he assumed without authority. The right of the people to keep and bear arms, shall not be infringed, says the Constitution; but upon this privilege he has trampled ·in Maryland, Missouri, and Kentucky. The right of the people peaceably to assemble and petition Government for a redress of grievances was equally inalienable; yet this right was abolished in New York by police intervention. So, "no warrant shall issue but upon probable cause;" but Mr. Lincoln procured the arrest of inoffensive citizens without *either* warrant or cause.* The same Constitution provides that in all criminal prosecutions the accused shall be informed of the nature and cause of accusation; *he* hurried hundreds to the dungeons of his prisons and denied to them

---

* As a single individual illustration of the Northern despotism, we will simply refer to the case of Mrs. Greenhow, the widow of the late Professor Greenhow, formerly principal translator in the United States Department of State. From a communication addressed by her to Secretary Seward, we make the following extract: "I most respectfully submit, that on Friday, August 23rd, without warrant or other show of authority, I was arrested by the Detective Police, and my house taken in charge by them; that all my private letters, and papers of a life-time, were read and examined by them: that every law of decency was violated in the search of my house and person, and by the surveillance over me. We read in history, that the poor Maria Antoinette had a paper torn from her bosom by lawless hands, and that even a change of linen had to be effected in sight of her brutal captors. It is my sad *experience* to record even more revolting outrages than that, for during the first days of my imprisonment, whatever *necessity* forced me to seek my chamber, a detective stood sentinel at the open door. And thus, for a period of seven days, I, with my little child, was placed absolutely at the mercy of men without character or responsibility; that during the first evening, a portion of these men became brutally drunk, and boasted in my hearing of the "*nice times*" they expected to have, with the female prisoners; and that rude violence was used towards a colored servant girl during that evening, the extent of which I have not been able to learn. For any show of decorum afterwards practised towards me, I was indebted to the Detective called Captain Dennis." Mrs. Greenhow adds, that in her own house, which has been converted into her prison, a public prostitute is lodged and supported by the Federal Government.

the benefits of this provision. It guaranteed that no person should be held guilty of treason, unless on the testimony of two witnesses to the same overt act, or on confession in open court; but without evidence, authority of court, or form of trial, *he* has condemned and incarcerated men and women upon mere suspicion. It provided that in all criminal prosecutions, the accused should be entitled to the assistance of counsel for his defence; *he* has confined within the walls of a military fortress one of counsel for such prisoners (Algernon S. Sullivan;) and, although entitled to "a speedy and public trial by an impartial jury," he was never confronted by an accuser. By virtue of the eighth amendment to the Constitution, excessive bail should not be asked, excessive fines imposed, nor cruel and unusual punishments inflicted; yet Mr. Lincoln refuses to grant his victims trial—refuses to accept bail on their behalf—and has committed many of them to the cells invariably selected for murderers, notorious criminals, and incorrigible vagabonds. No person should be subject for the same offence, to be twice put in jeopardy of life or limb; but he has had citizens arrested and imprisoned, then discharged as guiltless, and afterwards rearrested and deprived of liberty. Congress was prohibited from making any law "abridging the freedom of speech or of the press;" he has stifled the freedom of speech, and suppressed the circulation of every newspaper of his section, which dared to condemn his policy. This has been the fate of the New York *Day Book, News, Journal of Commerce, Freeman's Journal*, Brooklyn *Eagle*, Philadelphia *Christian Observer*, Westchester (Pa.) *Jeffersonian*, Bridgeport (Conn.) *Farmer*, and a long catalogue of others. "The right of the people to be secure in their persons, houses, papers, and effects, against unreasonable searches and seizures, shall not be violated, and no warrants shall issue but upon probable cause, supported by oath or affirmation particularly describing the place to be searched, and the persons or things to be seized," was a solemn assurance of the Constitution. But he regarded it with scorn.

He had innocent men and women *seized* in the silent hours of night, by rude and drunken officers. He had houses—which are usually supposed to be castles of freemen—subjected to the unreasonable searches of a blackguard soldiery, fished, for the most part, from purlieus of vice and sinks of degradation. In the seizure of private papers, he went so far as to cause his marshals to make a concerted descent, at three o'clock on a certain afternoon, upon every considerable telegraph office within the compass of his rule, and grasp their accumulated dispatches for the preceding twelve months, with a view of ascertaining who were the Northern confidential correspondents of influential men in the Confederate States. "The whole matter was managed with the greatest secrecy, and so well planned that the project was a complete success," said his most unscrupulous organ next day, in announcing the consummation of the abominable manœuvre. And, to perfect the enslavement of those whom he rules, he had the writ of *habeas corpus* virtually abolished—that sacred privilege which carries the mind of the freeman back to the struggle at Runnymede, and weds the history of the present day to that of the Middle Age. It was provided by the Constitution that "the writ of habeas corpus should not be suspended, unless in cases of rebellion or invasion." The State of Maryland was not invaded, except by Federal soldiers; neither had she rebelled against the Government of the Union; yet, when one of her citizens—Mr. John Merriman—was illegally deprived of liberty, the venerable process, issued out in his behalf, and made returnable before the Chief Justice of the United States, who had administered the oath of office to the President, it was contemptuously spit upon by Mr. Lincoln, whose sworn duty it was to guard it; and in every Northern State this writ of freedom is now suspended!

But the tyranny of Mr. Lincoln did not stop with the oppression of individuals; he went so far as to render the hereditary rights of societies nugatory. "Full faith and credit," reads the Constitution, "shall be given in each State, to the public acts, records, and judicial proceedings of every other State." But the decrees of State Conventions; the enactments of State Legislatures; or the proceedings of State Courts, have been treated by him of less value than the paper upon which they were recorded. "Nothing in this Constitution," adds the same great Charter, "shall be so construed as to prejudice the claims of the *United States*, or of *any particular State*" to the territories of the Union. Not one foot of such soil shall ever be given up to the institutions of the Southern States, is the magisterial proclamation of Mr. Lincoln. "No preference shall be given by any regulations of commerce or revenue to the ports of one State over another; nor shall vessels, bound to or from one State, be obliged to enter, clear, or pay duties in another." His violation of this clause is positively sublime. He has already blockaded the ports and harbors of twelve sovereign States, and caused vessels bound to them, to change their course and enter into the ports of other States. "No new State shall be formed or erected within the jurisdiction of any other State; nor any State be formed by the junction of two more States, or parts of States, without the consent of the Legislatures of the States concerned, as well as of the Congress," reads the noble treaty: but Mr. Lincoln and his Government, without the consent of any Legislature, have endeavored to erect a new State out of the disloyal counties of Western Virginia, and are now laboring to " form a junction " of the counties of Northumberland and Accomac, Va., with the State of Delaware. The Constitution provides, that " the citizens of each State shall be entitled to *all* the privileges and immunities of citizens in the several States." But to be a citizen of a Southern State, without being a sworn traitor to birth-right, is a sufficient cause for imprisonment and confiscation of property, at the North. The war-making power was vested in Congress only, yet, without its sanction, or any other legal authority whatever, Mr. Lincoln made war upon the Confederate States. All and every State were prohibited, without the consent of Congress, from engaging in war, unless *actually* invaded or in imminent danger. But without invasion, or danger of invasion, he induced most of the States to make war upon the others. The power of, or right in, the Federal Government, to invade or coerce a State, was refused to the Constitution by those, the work of whose souls it was; yet the world beholds to-day the strange spectacle of fourteen sovereignties invaded, or in actual danger of invasion. An army of subjugation is upon Virginia's soil; the tramp of the oppressor's heel is heard upon an inlet of North Carolina; and while these lines are writing, the roar of the invader's cannon calls to arms the sons of the little Spartan State of Jackson and Calhoun.

In Missouri, unparalleled outrages were, and are still being perpetrated. The dignity of the Commonwealth was grossly insulted. Her people were stripped of their natural rights and liberties. The solemn enactments of her Legislature were nullified and ridiculed. Her militia was disarmed, persecuted, and arrested. Her commerce was suppressed. Her newspapers were silenced. Her children were placed under the espionage of unprincipled men, and handed over to the ruthless mercilessness of an armed soldiery. Her best sons were imprisoned—debarred from the pleasures of home, native fields, and the sweet wooings of Nature—without crime and without warrant; and unoffending women and children were barbarously murdered, or shot down like quarry, in her cities. Finally, the State was declared under martial law!

Passing over the fields laid waste—the towns and villages razed or burned—the property stolen or destroyed—the churches desecrated and women ravished, in Virginia; we come to Kentucky—a State claimed to be still in the Union. Unfortunately for this chivalrous Commonwealth, while influenced by the concerted advice of timid men and false teachers, she resolved upon being an impossibility : she would be neutral, that she might impartially mediate between the unnatural belligerents. But the advocates of neutrality were to her, what Æschines was to Athens—foxes in the habiliments of lambs. *He* was secretly in league with Philip ; *they* were secretly in league with Abraham. They promised fair things—they used specious arguments—they glozed like the serpent, and like the serpent they betrayed. Under the plea of self-protection, they had arms surreptitiously placed in the hands of traitors to be used against neighbors and fellow-men.   Growing bold with temporary success, they had paid mercenaries introduced into, and Federal camps established upon, the soil of their own State; the neck of which, by a desperate and cunning stroke, they endeavored to place in the mouth of the wolf.   But the people at length awoke and found that they were entrapped.   They beheld their Legislature partly venal, partly treacherous, and partly intimidated by military bayonets.   They saw that the independent press of their State was either muzzled or silenced. They witnessed loyal citizens hunted like deer or wild fowl, and compelled to seek an asylum of safety in exile. They heard of the arrest at the hour of midnight of eminent and patriotic statesmen*—men who were vene-

---

* From a newspaper, in the interest of Mr. Lincoln, the Cincinnati *Commercial*, we gather the following: "Colonel Connell and other officers visited Judge Jackson—one of the bitterest secessionists in Knox county, Ky.   He is wealthy and influential, and distinguished himself recently by hospitality to Zollicoffer and his officers, but declined to call upon the Federal officers.   Col. Connell and Lieutenant Colonel Spears, of the First (Federal) Tennessee Regiment, concluded to visit him.   They called at night, and the family, supposing they came to arrest the Judge, were much distressed. * * * * After fumbling about the house for some time a member of the family found a Bible, and the oath was administered with threatening emphasis to Jackson.   The Judge was required to place his hand on the Bible, and Spears dictated to him the extremest minutiæ of an oath, which covered the ground entirely, and closed by exclaiming: 'And so, in the name of Almighty God, you do solemnly swear, as you hope for salvation, that you will true allegiance bear to the Government of the United States, *without equivocation or mental reservation*.'   When the Judge responded affirmatively, Spears ordered him to *kiss* the Bible. The former demurred that the oath was not administered in Kentucky in that way.   Spears replied he ' didn't care a g—d d—n what they did in Kentucky, the Bible must be kissed,' and it was."

And this but a single instance, in illustration of a general and vulgar tyranny.

11

rable from age, and distinguished as public servants during an ordinary lifetime; but whose hands were now pinioned before them, like criminals of ages long past, and carried captive to a military prison in New York, one thousand miles from their homes! But there is a limit to endurance. Young Kentucky took fire and revolted; and that unfortunate State is now precipitated, through the machinations and usurpations of Mr. Lincoln, into a bloody revolution, likely to be unequalled, perhaps, but by one terrible exception, in the annals of history.

In Maryland—unhappy Maryland—his crimes have been still more enormous. There, his uniformed ruffians, in the very dawn of the contest, shot down harmless and defenceless spectators. He had the municipal government of the city of Baltimore subverted. He had the mayor stripped of his legal authority. He had the chief of police, Marshal Kane, arrested and imprisoned. He had the board of police commissioners abolished, and the old police force substituted by a corps of men, many of whose portraits had previously been ornaments in "the rogues' gallery." These base hirelings, without warrant or other judicial sanction, invaded the sanctuaries of private dwellings, seized private papers, carried away private property, and arrested inoffensive men. They made war upon the texture of ladies' dresses and children's clothes, when their colors approximated to those of the Confederate flag. The people were disarmed. The State was garrisoned by a Federal force of between thirty-five and forty thousand men, in three divisions, respectively commanded by Generals Banks, Sickles, and Dix.

Nathaniel P. Banks, of Massachusetts, is a man whose

political life commenced as a democrat, but being governed by a sordid ambition, he soon became wearied of laboring with an unprofitable minority, and veered with every change of the popular compass, until he was made a general of division by President Lincoln. Daniel E. Sickles, of New York, is a *person* of yet more unenviable fame. In youth he was the favored pensioner of a notorious and dashing harlot; in manhood, for personal preferment, he pandered—infamously on his part, and dishonorably on the part of his wife—to the depraved appetites of men in high places; and to this he ' afterwards added a premeditated, cold-blooded, and calculating assassination. John A. Dix has had the advantages of a tolerable education and good social intercourse; but Nature made him hollow-hearted, cunning, selfish, parsimonious, ungenerous, ungrateful, and unprincipled. His life-Odyssey has been that of a place-hunter. In 1848, he deserted the Democratic party, and, by rebellion, helped to bring upon it disaster and defeat. Next, he professed penitence, and was once more received into its folds; and now we find him allied to his hereditary political foes, an avenging scourge in the service of Abraham Lincoln.

The wrongs inflicted upon a peculiarly sensitive and high-spirited people, by a ribald and undisciplined soldiery, so officered, may be more easily conceived than described.* They are subjected daily to insult and

---

* Dr. William Howard Russell, special correspondent of the London *Times*, in one of his recent letters to that world-renowned journal, says: "Let the members of the English club picture such a scene as this. A body of men in plain clothes march up to the steps, forbid any one to leave the house, place guards in the hall, take the keys out

abuse—to rapine and murder. Many of the most opulent and estimable sons of Maryland, upon mere suspicion, or to gratify private malice, have been torn from
their families, and consigned to loathsome dungeons.
The writ of *Habeas Corpus* has been suspended in their
midst, and the courts rendered powerless to protect
them. The poor of Baltimore have been deprived of
the daily rations, supplied to them by the Christian
munificence of their fellow-citizen, Ross Winans, who
was rewarded for his charity, by Mr. Lincoln, with a
cell in a military fortress. General Dix has leveled his
cannon at the devoted city, from forts, camps, and en-
trenchments, with the promise to lay it into ashes in
case of an attack being made upon him by the Confederates. During the sitting of the State Convention,
fearful that it might pass an ordinance of secession, he
watched its proceedings like a martinet, and, with the
clangor of surrounding arms, intimidated its members;
as the notorious Major Sirr sought to intimidate the
celebrated Celtic advocate, while defending one of "the
United Irishmen." Finally, he had the members of the
State Legislature, supposed to be loyal to the South,

---

of the doors, proceed to tear up the floors, to disturb the cellars and
throw over the coals—refuse to show any warrant to any of the members, and merely state that they are looking for concealed arms by
authority of the marshal, and then leave as they came, without the
production of warrant, or showing in dress, uniform or badge, that
they are really constables, or employed by any authority whatever.
And yet this is what took place at the Maryland Club in Baltimore the
day of my arrival—a club of the most respectable gentlemen in the
State—without a word of excuse, explanation or apology. It is not
perverting hospitality, nor is it hostility to republican institutions, to
condemn such acts as these."

banished or imprisoned, so as to prevent the meeting of that representative body.*

Thus was every vestige of liberty and security to the citizen overthrown — thus were municipal rights cancelled and destroyed—and thus was State sovereignty obliterated by Abraham Lincoln—a man whose sworn obligations were, to protect and preserve each and all— a man who, were it not beneath the dignity of history, one might, in the language of Curran, brand as "the perjurer of an hundred oaths," who blasts the memory of the dead, blights the hopes of the living, and measures his greatness upon the ruin of his country and the graves of his victims.

But the melancholy feature of this picture is in the singular attitude assumed by the people of the North. It has been severely said of the Scotch, that they sold their king and country for a pittance, which amounted but to four pence a head, for each of their population. If this were truth, and not fiction, surely the conduct of our present adversaries would put the disgraceful transaction in the shade ; for in forfeiting their liberties, they have gained nothing and lost every thing. Accustomed to decry and defame all other governments but their own — accustomed to weep over the fate of Greece, Poland, and Hungary—accustomed to espouse the cause

---

* No wonder, then, that Lord Lyons, H. B. Majesty's Minister at Washington, in a dispatch to William II. Seward, should have characterized the Lincoln Government as a "despotic and arbitrary power," which "refused to pay obedience to the writ of *habeas corpus*," and the "irregular proceedings" of which are "contrary to the maxims of the United States." Indeed, the only wonder is, that wretched government has not earned for itself the contempt of all civilized mankind.

of Lombardy and Venetia against Austria, the cause of the Papal States against the Pope — they have voted thousands, reckoned by hundreds, of men, and millions of money, to support a despotism, compared with which, those of King Bomba and Francis Joseph were balm; in order to crush out a people who keep the vestal flame alive, kindled by Washington and Jefferson!

> "There is the moral of all human tales;
> 'Tis but the same rehearsal of the past,
> First Freedom, and then Glory—when that fails,
> Wealth, vice, corruption,—barbarism at last.
> And History, with all her volumes vast,
> Hath but *one* page."

Justice may be compatible with Monarchy, but never with Tyranny. The tyrant feels that Justice can always be disputed by Force, and he relies upon the power of the latter to wring submission from weakness. The Northern Government felt that justice and right were on the side of the South, but, in the consciousness of possessing numbers, brute force, an organized army and navy, bullion and established authority, it eschewed these facts. Secession, indeed, was revolution; but it was unlike any other revolution of history; it was a revolution of opinion, not the work of an individual or of a political party, but the natural result and spontaneous desire of a magnanimous people; it was a revolution without a leader, yet a revolution in which all men were leaders—rendering it impossible to sacrifice any one man for an assumed political crime, where all men were alike criminal; it was born of homogeneous sentiments, and designed as a resisting barrier of ancient rights and habits, against the contagious encroachments and aggression of new modes of thought in heterogeneous forces; and the height of its Christian ambition was to be bloodless. The South supplicated the North for peace—to borrow the language of Ariosto—in words "which might for pity stop the passing sun." Past memories were invoked by the former; she appealed to reason; she argued that a Union not founded upon principles of mutual rectitude and benevolence, and not cemented by bonds of love, was unworthy of the name and could not stand; yet, upon the ruins of the structure, men of a common lineage, a common tongue, and a common heritage of historic patriotism, might still meet upon terms of kindliness and amity, and pursue, albeit by two different paths, a common career toward a destiny of greatness and splendor. But all this moderation and good faith were answered by threats and execrations: the North resolved upon a policy of blood and carnage— a policy beneath the social economy of animal instinct, and, therefore, unworthy of being termed *brutal*. For he who will enter some fine zoological garden—who will mark the conduct and intercourse of the varied creatures congregated there together—study their leagues of tender and generous friendships—see how they accommodate themselves to the circumstances of their new condition—and then compare their virtuous alliance with the barbarous war-fury of the North, will hesitate to rank the *human* with the *brutal* government. We have seen children at a menagerie, cultivate with crackers and sweetmeats the friendship of grizzly bears; but the generous leniency of the South served only to lash the North into savage blood-thirstiness. And surely the sociological machinery whereby Nature regulates the harmony of Barnum's "happy family," is higher in the scale of moral self-government, than that by which the people of the latter section seek to force the former into submission—the boom of the cannon, the click of the rifle, and the point of the bayonet. But the contrast does not cease here. The lordly lion will roar when in quest of prey; the rattle-snake will warn its victim before it poisons; man alone assassinates; and the North endeavored to lull the South into a slumber of confidence, with the intention of then strangling her.

XVII.

Soon after the inauguration of Mr. Lincoln, and the organization of his administration, the Confederate Government deputed an embassy of three commissioners to Washington, authorized to negotiate for the removal of the Federal garrisons from fortresses Pickens and Sumter. Their mission was friendly, humane, and amicable; they were clothed with power, by the seven seceded States, to form a new alliance with what remained of the United States—directed to sacrifice every thing but honor and independence, in order to avoid the horrors of civil war, prevent the shedding of fraternal gore, and perpetuate the blessings of amity to the whole continent. In the discharge of this sacred and philanthropic duty, they promptly addressed a communication, which explained the functions of the embassy and its purposes, to the Federal Secretary of State, William H. Seward.

Now, this professional politician is to diplomacy, what Ahmad Khamàkin, the arch-thief of the Oriental tale—

who could break through the outer wall, scale the inner
one, and steal Kohl from the eye of the sleeper—was to
burglary. He declined to return an official answer to
the communication of the Confederate commissioners;
because, as he alleged, the political party which elevated
him to power (upon the ruins of a broken Constitution
and dismembered country), regarded them as "rebels,"
and to so treat with them might *then* seriously embarrass
the administration of Mr. Lincoln. His public policy
was always founded upon the philosophy of example,
from which he did not now depart in resorting to duplicity—he found an inglorious precedent in two strokes
of dishonest artfulness, practised during the last days
of President Buchanan's administration. Like Seward,
Buchanan's life is but the story of an office-seeker, growing rich in his vocation, and finally raised to the highest
civic honors, through Southern patronage. Politicians
are seldom grateful, and he proved no exception to the
rule. Like the traitor son of Carioth, he sought to
reward his benefactors by betrayal. When the State of
South Carolina seceded, her authorities resolved to take
possession of the forts in Charleston harbor. To prevent this and gain time, he promised to negotiate—
promised that the existing *status* of those fortifications
should not be disturbed; yet he caused Major Anderson, in the dead hour of night, to *steal* his men out of
Fort Moultrie into Fort Sumter—spiking the cannon,
burning the gun carriages, and destroying, generally,
the public property in the former fortress, ere it was
deserted. From this moment forward, Mr. Buchanan's
career became more and more unconstitutional and un-
American. Many of his ablest advisers were constrained
to withdraw from his cabinet; amongst them, John B.

Floyd, Secretary of War. To fill his place, Buchanan selected Joseph Holt, a man born upon Southern soil, but to the South what Benedict Arnold was to the Revolution. When the position of the garrison in Fort Sumter became untenable, he and his master vainly resolved upon secretly reinforcing it. This resolution was not only skilfully concealed from other members of the cabinet, but the Secretary of the Interior—Hon. Jacob Thompson—was positively assured that no such attempt would be made without his knowledge. In a few days, however, after the receipt of such a pledge, and early in the month of January, he learned from the newspapers that a steamship called "The Star of the West," with provisions, munitions of war, and two hundred and fifty armed men on board, had been dispatched from the harbor of New York upon so infamous a mission!

Although both of these fraudulent measures turned out to be miserable abortions, they were accepted as sufficient precedents to guide and shape the policy of Mr. Seward. But while declining to respond to the Southern embassy, like his predecessors, he affected great depression of spirits in private circles, and whispered that he completely inclined to accede, in due time, to their wishes. In a conversation of this character, with Justice Nelson, of the United States Supreme Court, he pitifully enlarged upon his embarrassments, but asserted his determination to save the sections from an armed collision. The generous and sincere are seldom incredulous or suspicious, and moved by these representations, the former induced one of his colleagues upon the bench—Justice John A. Campbell—to accompany him upon a visit to the latter. The meeting took place—the three alone were present. Mr. Seward's "depression" and oppression, arising from the fact that the Southern Commissioners pressed him for a reply to their message, were made painfully manifest. He gave his visitors the most solemn and positive assurances that his disposition was entirely pacific. He told them that there would be no attempt made to reinforce Fort Pickens. He gave them to understand that in five days' time the Federal troops would be removed from Fort Sumter. Judge Campbell, at the time, held in his hand a draft of a letter which he proposed addressing to President Davis, at Montgomery: "before that letter reaches its destination," observed the veracious Seward, "Sumter will have been evacuated." This was on the 15th of March; and with such gratifying assurances, the humane and learned Judge became a voluntary intermediary. He hastened to the room of one of the Commissioners— Judge Crawford—and communicated to him the happy intelligence. The cheering news soon ran from lip to lip, and every face in Washington beamed with gladness and fresh hopes.

But the five days passed, and Sumter was *not* evacuated; while the officer in command was making repairs and putting it in a condition of aggression and defence. The same intermediary called again upon the Secretary of State, and the latter reiterated his former assurances. These were communicated at once to the Embassy—to President Davis; to Governor Pickens, of S. C.; and to General Beauregard. To rock the South into a more perfect sleep of security, Colonel Lamon—an agent of the Lincoln Government—was sent to Charleston. He informed Governor Pickens that he was authorized to make arrangements for the withdrawal of the Federal troops from Sumter, and proposed a vessel of war as the best means of effecting this; which was, of course, very properly declined. Another confidential agent of Mr. Lincoln's, one Fox, was soon afterwards dispatched to the same city. He requested permission to visit Fort Sumter, solemnly asseverating that his mission was entirely pacific; and through the intervention of a gallant naval officer, Captain Hartstene, his wish was complied with. But Fox shamelessly violated his faith, and reported to Major Anderson a plan agreed upon by the unscrupulous Washington Government, for the forcible reinforcement of the Fort; in accordance with which, a naval fleet was being manned, provisioned and fitted out in the harbor of New York. All these facts having become matter of newspaper notoriety, Judge Campbell addressed a note, on the seventh day of April, to Secretary Seward, to which the latter laconically replied: "FAITH AS TO SUMTER FULLY KEPT—WAIT AND SEE." And he imparted similar assurances to Mr. Harvey, now his own Minister at the Court of Lisbon. Finally, a Mr. Chew and a Lieutenant Talbot were sent by Mr. Lincoln to Governor Pickens, with a paper informing him that the Fort *should* be supplied and reinforced! This was the consummation of governmental perfidy, perhaps unparalleled in history, except in the violation of the Treaty of Limerick by William of Orange. Justice Campbell did "wait and see faith as to Sumter" so "fully kept," that on the 13th of April—on the sixth day after Seward's pledge was given—a hostile Federal fleet menace Charleston—causing Confederate guns to open fire upon the Fortress, and compelling its commander to surrender; without the loss of a single Confederate life, while the fleet made an inglorious retreat.

But thus, by the deception, duplicity, Sejanus-faced, and wicked policy of President Lincoln and William H. Seward, was kindled the torch of discord and civil war— the lurid glare of which reddens thousands of miles to-day, and arrays in deadly fray a million of men.

No sooner had Sumter fallen than the authors of the war raised their visors. Lincoln called into the field seventy-five thousand men, "to crush rebellion." He sent his hireling emissaries all over the North, inciting the people to madness—preaching the holiness of a crusade against the South. Public meetings were convened in villages, towns, and cities, at all and each of which the tocsin of war was sounded. The largest of these was held in the city of New York—always famous for cheap or easily improvised pageants. Heartless demagogues, like "Colonel" John Cochrane*—one who could (as he really did) coolly advocate, in a laboriously written speech, his own election to Congress, at the very moment when the shroud was being put upon the remains of his deceased parent—harangued the multi-

---

*In a speech recently delivered by this officer, he is reported to have said: "Shall we not seize the cotton at Beaufort, the munitions of war? And if you would seize their property, open their ports, and even destroy their lives, I ask you whether you would not use their slaves? whether you would not arm their slaves [great applause], and carry them in battalions against their masters? [Renewed and tumultuous applause.] If necessary to save this Government, I would plunge their whole country, black and white, in one indiscriminate sea of blood, so that we should, in the end, have a government which would be the vicegerent of God." "Col." Cochrane is nephew to Gerritt Smith—one of the bloodiest of abolitionists— and certainly not unworthy of his uncle's adoration; especially as the doctrines propounded above have been fully endorsed by Simon Cameron, United States Secretary of War.

tude. He had for coadjutors on that occasion, other men, whom, to describe, were to pollute the vocabulary of the English tongue. They denounced and reviled the South, and pledged their section to the support of their President. Lincoln summoned his obsequious Congress; it assembled; stifled free discussion; ignored the Constitution; voted him millions of money; munitions of war; and placed over half a million of base hirelings at his disposal. For weeks, the work of preparation went bravely on. The music of fife and drum was heard all over the Northern States. The enthusiasm of their people was rampant. *Their* forts, *their* guns, *their* arsenals, were to be summarily recovered: everything now belonged to *them;* the South could claim *no part* of that public property which was held in common by all under the old partnership. Mr. Lincoln seized upon the mint, upon the army and navy, upon the fortifications, custom houses, and light-houses; upon every element of power within his reach; and in the vain conceit of invincibility, he promised to his deluded followers, the subjugation of the seceded States. He called upon the people of the North to uphold his banner; they obeyed; surrendered their liberties without murmur; and like tigers, thirsted for the blood of former friends, fellow-citizens, and relations. They were told that they would be led by "the greatest General of the age—Winfield Scott;" that the rebels would be extirpated; their estates and property confiscated; and that the booty should reward Northern valor. Like those who, in a darker era and a better cause, followed Peter the Hermit, they crowded to the standard of this base, unprincipled, and avaricious traitor—the Wellington of the "Old Dominion," and to her what the Iron Duke was to Ireland—a renegade and traitor. This incarnate personation of Vanity, was born and educated in Virginia; and the old cavalier State heaped upon him honor after honor, in return for which he led his mercenary hordes to desecrate her soil, and strip her children of their liberties; as an ingrate son would *sell* his mother's chastity into the polluted embraces of a debaucher! But Nemesis is sometimes just; and she now lashes him with serpents of awakened Conscience, in defeat, humiliation, and disgrace, a wanderer and an exile—the victim of loathsome diseases, while the worm of remorse, like the vulture of Tityus, forever gnaws upon his cold and ungenial heart.

It may not be uninteresting to glance now at the fruit of Mr. Lincoln's and his advisers' policy.

When Fort Sumter was surrendered, and when *he* issued his war proclamation, the Southern Confederacy was composed of seven sovereign States only. But that document thrilled through the Southern heart—roused its patriotic emotions—and quickened into armed resistance, its gallantry and chivalry. The Governors of nearly all of the unseceded slave States, responded in terms of defiance and disgust, to the demand made upon them by the Northern Secretary of War, for contingent troops. Arkansas, North Carolina, Virginia, and Tennessee, promptly withdrew from the Government of the invader and oppressor, and pitched their future destinies with the new Republic. The great State of Missouri, in the very teeth of outrage, invasion, and military tyranny, has recently emulated their heroic example. And Kentucky has resolved not " to lay her lovely forehead in the dust:" she is boldly, fearlessly, and rapidly marching in the same congenial direction.

But notwithstanding such acquisitions, immediate or

anticipated, the disparity between the populations of both sections and their aggressive resources, was remarkable, and to all but the brave and resolute, disheartening. The North boasted of a population of twenty millions of souls; the South could not number ten millions. The North had a floating populace, the South had not. In the North there were wandering classes, ever ready for wild or lawless adventure—desperate persons, whose principal profession was crime. There, also, the great tide of European immigration settled; and the great majority of immigrants support their families from the wages of their daily toil. To coerce these dependents into military service, all conceivable and reckless artifices were resorted to. General enterprise ceased; public works were stopped; private charities were suspended, or forcibly suppressed; and liberal promises made (which were never fulfilled) that the families of those who enlisted, and were needful, should be plentifully and gratuitously supported. Accustomed to follow the lead, in many a well-fought political battle, of such men as Edward Everett and Daniel S. Dickinson, the people now found themselves without a leader; for these leaders, and all of their trading class, had, strangely enough, become rabid supporters of the Lincoln policy. The democratic masses, who helped to support upon their brawny shoulders the pillars of the Union, soon found themselves without an organ of opinion; for their customary newspapers were overpowered or crushed out of existence. The Northern President and his Cabinet—their itinerant rhetoricians upon the rostrum—the slavish press which was spared from persecution, the violence of mob-law, and the tortures of constrained silence—and ministers of the Gospel, characteristically raised from the anvil or the lapstone, to sacerdotal dignity, yet ignorant of spiritual religion, church history, and scientific theology—all these forces, like Mexican priests, joined in an harmonious psalm of blood-thirstiness, preparatory to their contemplated offering, in human sacrifice of the volunteer patriots of the South! The heterogeneous elements of a conglomerated society were invoked to forget former prejudices, old contentions, and present animosities; and to unite in one grand league for one grand purpose. A political party, which had shamelessly and clandestinely labored to betray our country during its second war with England; which had recklessly and persistently sought to bring disgrace and defeat upon its arms in the Mexican war; now prayed democrats to drink of the cup of oblivion—to make war upon those who had ever been loyal, even at the expense of their best blood and treasure—and this time, to associate with recreants and fanatics, in a crusade for the honor, forsooth! of a flag which symbolized their nationality. Irishmen were informed, by those who had strenuously tried to disfranchise them; who had burned their churches; who had derided and insulted their branch of the human race; who had outraged the devotees of their faith; and who, in many quarters, had laid their settlements in ashes and ruin; that this civil war was waged to give them a country, to perpetuate their political freedom, and to secure forever their personal liberties. Germans, fresh from the thraldom of their thirty tyrants, and but imperfectly acquainted with our language, were indoctrinated into a belief, that they were called upon to fight in defence of the privileges for which they had crossed the Atlantic—that upon their success in the contest rested their only hopes of free homesteads—and

12
.

that by the abolition of Southern slavery, they would become the possessors of Southern farms, or the recipients of Southern wages. In this manner—by such insinuations and misrepresentations, were gross dissimilarities reconciled—the worst passions of men excited—their wild aspirations stimulated—and their cupidity and avarice tempted. The more effectually to delude them, they were confidently taught that the North need show but a firm' and united front, to cause the South, broken and divided, to succumb; and that even if it came to blows, the war would be simply "short, sharp, and decisive:" for to completely subjugate the latter, was merely a holiday entertainment.

Thus was created an agitation, at once artificial and fanatical, by means of which, before the middle of June, Mr. Lincoln found himself commander-in-chief of an army of not less than three hundred thousand men; the best appointed and equipped, it was boasted, ever brought into the field of action. Their muskets, their rifles, their revolvers, and their artillery, were of the finest quality and of the most approved inventions. They had all accessories of convenience and advantage—the greatest commanders in the world; rail-cars; steamboats; and shipping, for transportation—the best telescopes and the most wonderful *balloons*, for purposes of observation. Their cannon was so long, of such awful range and terrific roar, that, like the magic horn of Astolpho, it would put the enemy to flight, in confusion and dismay. And as to the physical material of which the "grand army" was composed, that, of course, was unquestioned and unquestionable. Although it was baptized after *the* grand army of Napoleon I., the prowess of the Gaul could not be compared with the *peculiar*

bravery of a soldiery which had been distinguished as
manufacturers of shoe pegs, washing machines, apple
peeling machines, patent locks, patent churns, and other
ingeniously useful devices of New England mechanism.
Besides, the major portion of them belonged to the home
militia and excursion target companies, of the North;
and they were disciplined. On holidays, they made a
splendid show in their respective cities; dressed themselves in fancifully variegated regimentals; their left
feet promptly responding to the "hep" of the orderly
sergeant. They went through the formulas of sham
battles, and "regulars" could have done no more; hence
they were *soldiers* and invincible. And now that they
were to meet a real foe, face to face, the *fe*, *fi*, *fo*, *fum*
of the giant in the nursery tale, could not equal their
sublimity of contempt for him. Their vaunts were heard
over Europe and America. Rebellion was not only to
be suppressed at home, but ere Lincolndom would put
down its arms, corpulent and "perfidious" John Bull
should be honored with a coat of tar and feathers, after
the most approved Yankee notion.

But the race is not always to the swift, nor the battle
to the strong. The loudest boaster may frequently be
made to bite the dust, in ignominy and defeat. This
was the lesson which David taught Goliah—which Miltiades inculcated at Marathon—which Themistocles enforced in the bay of Salamis—which Packenham learned
at New Orleans—which the Swiss imparted to Charles
of Burgundy—which immortalizes Cambus Kenneth
and Bannockburn. The mercenaries of the tyrant have
never yet hopelessly conquered the soldiers of Justice—
a truth which, so far, has been fully evinced in the success of our arms.

The North, however, clamored for an advance, for she had set her heart upon a great success with which to redeem her fading fortunes. She demanded that a terrible blow should be inflicted, and that the overture to extirpation should have a bloody opening. One of her newspaper heroes, Gen. Butler, commanded at Fortress Monroe; and in obedience to the prevailing sentiment, he ordered, early in June, Gen. Pierce, with five regiments numbering four thousand men, to march upon Great Bethel. They were confronted by eleven hundred Confederates under the intrepid Magruder, who drove them back, routed, slaughtered, and decimated. They left upon the field of action two hundred of their companions in arms, while our loss was but one killed and three wounded! This was a foretaste of the hospitality with which invaders and marauders were to be greeted by Southern prowess. But those who held the hounds in leash were not contented—they beat their breasts, like furious gorillas, and cried out for revenge. The contending forces met again, beneath a burning July sun, at Bull Run. Gen. Longstreet's brigade of Confederates, aided by the N. O. Washington Artillery, repulsed a force of Federals, numbering perhaps three to one. The drama of Bethel was reënacted; five hundred of the enemy were put *hors de combat;* while our loss, in killed and wounded, did not exceed eighty.

Louder, and more defiant than before, now roared the bellicose North. Humiliation and defeat had not taught her wisdom. Her President had previously given the rebels thirty days to disperse and return to their homes; but his proclamation was derided and disobeyed. Her venal and subsidized journals demanded that the people of the South should be given as a

retributive breakfast, to satiate the revenge of her
mercenaries and their generals. " On to Richmond "
was their favorite watchword. " The greatest Captain
of the Age " was ordered to put his invincible corps in
motion ; and he responded that he was ready to suppress
secession—that he was prepared to convince the world
that Washington contained " a Government "—and
that, like an immature egg in the palm of his hand, he
had "rebellion" in his power. The whole North was
full of unctuous grace, and offered thanks to its peculiar
God—the *golden* calf; Puritan and Quaker knelt side
by side in prayer ; and rising, sung to the tune of *Old
Hundred :*

> "Woe! Woe! to the Rebels," etc.

Gen. Scott having matured his plan of battle, ordered
Gen. McDowell, at the head of fifty-five thousand men,
to advance on Manassas, July 21st—three days after
the repulse at Bull Run. As they advanced, the gay
uniforms of the Federal ranks, their streaming colors
and bristling bayonets, added strange charms to the primeval forests of Virginia. Fair dames; members of
Congress; women of pleasure; and men of leisure, all in
costly and rich attire, brought up the rear of the seemingly grand holiday procession. In show, splendid boast,
and dramatic accessories, it was no mean theatrical rep-
resentation of the army of Xerxes. In martial strains
the noble trumpet resounded in front, while hearts of
roe, in serried columns, marched behind, chaunting :

> "Old John Brown lies a mouldering in his grave,
>   Hallelujah, Hallelujah,
>   Hallelujah, Hallelujah,
> Old John Brown lies a mouldering in his grave,
> But his soul is marching on."

Senator Wilson, of Massachusetts, was among the camp-followers and spectators. He commenced life a cobbler by trade; he afterwards deserted the awl and lapstone for the profession of a politician, and succeeded in "making money;" with a portion of which he now patronized the Vieuve Clicquot, Moet and Chandon, Jules Mumm, and Charles Heidsick, preparatory to his giving a great festival after the Federal victory. The "grand army" was provided with every means that Yankee ingenuity could devise for its success, with bloodhounds to discover "the rebels," and thirty thousand handcuffs to bind them when captured. So, early in the the morning, ere the sun could have sipped the dews of night, Lincolndom commenced the attack—at a safe and distant range. They were met by thirty-five thousand Southern patriots, defending their homes and freedom, and commanded by Generals Johnston and Beauregard— brave, skillful and modest officers. As our soldiers retired to more advantageous grounds, the Federal commanders telegraphed to headquarters, and headquarters to the Atlantic and Western cities, that they had achieved a signal victory. Men propose, but God disposes; and Senator Wilson, who had never dreamt even of defeat, had spread upon groaning tables his costly dinner. But 'twas partaken of by braver men than those for whom it was designed. The wisest of Greeks once told the wealthiest of Lydians, that a people with swords in their hands, would take his gold; so, on this occasion, Confederate soldiers dined at the expense of a vaunting enemy. For at four o'clock in the afternoon, the Federal hosts were in full flight—retreating in such confusion as army never fled before. It was the most terrible of recorded panics. Men fell down from sheer exhaustion and perished. Others were trodden to death beneath the hooves of flying horses, or crushed under the wheels of wagons and ambulances. Mr. Russell, correspondent of the London *Times*, an eye-witness of the scene, relates that the current of advancing and retreating Federal soldiery "met in wild disorder. 'Turn back, retreat!' shouted the men from the front, 'We're whipped, we're whipped.' They cursed and tugged at the horses' heads, and struggled with frenzy to get passed." "Men," he continued, "literally screamed with terror and fright, when their way was blocked up. On I rode, asking all, 'what is this all about?' and now and then, but rarely, receiving the answer, 'we're whipped' or 'we're repulsed.' Faces black and dusty, tongues out in the heat, eyes staring—it was a most wonderful sight. On they came like him

> Who, having turned, goes on
> And turns no more his head,
> For he knoweth that a fearful fiend
> Doth close behind him tread."

Some of the Federal fugitives never halted until they entered the city of Washington—thirty miles from the scene of action. Others sought shelter and protection in the woods, and were afterwards discovered half dead from terror and starvation. Many retreated on the road leading to Leesburg, and were captured. But the main body scampered in the direction of Arlington and Alexandria, leaving over five thousand of their comrades upon the field, and bearing with them two pieces only of the splendid artillery with which they advanced. In addition to fifty-six guns, some of which are of the heaviest calibre and longest range, twelve thousand stand of light arms, great quantities of blankets and clothing, medicine chests, provisions and munitions of war, sufficient to maintain for months a large army, fell into our hands—the princely donation, on the plains of Manassas, of the Northern Sennacherib to Israel.

In Missouri, the success of our arms was no less auspicious—there, too, Federalism was taught that the road of invasion was no path of roses. At Oak Hill, ten miles from Springfield, twelve thousand men, commanded by Gen. Lyon—a cruel and remorseless monster, but a zealous and energetic officer—assailed an encampment of ten thousand Confederates under General McCulloch. The battle raged with great bravery and desperation six-and-a-half hours, when the Federal forces were defeated, with a loss of eight hundred killed, one thousand wounded, three hundred prisoners, six pieces of artillery, and several hundred stand of small arms captured. Amongst the slain were Gen. Lyon and several of his prominent officers. Our loss, in killed, wounded and missing, was ten hundred and ninety-five! Next, and in a few weeks later, General Sterling Price attacked the enemy—commanded by Col. Mulligan, an honorable, brave, and gallant officer—in his fortifications at Lexington, Missouri, and after a continuous assault of fifty-two hours, with a loss of twenty-five killed and seventy-two wounded on our side, caused him to surrender. "The visible fruits of this victory"—to quote the language of General Price's official report—"were, about 3,500 prisoners, among whom are Colonels Mulligan, Marshall, Peabody, White, Grover, Major Van Horn, and 118 other commissioned officers, five pieces of artillery and two mortars, over 3,000 stand of infantry arms, a large number of sabres, about 750 horses, many.

sets of cavalry equipments, wagons, teams, ammunition, more than $100,000 worth of commissary stores, and a large amount of other property. In addition to all this, I obtained the restoration of the Great Seal of the State, of the public records, which had been stolen from their proper custodian, and about $900,000 in money, of which the bank of this place had been robbed, and which I have caused to be returned to it."

Indeed, so great, and singularly remarkable, have been the almost unbroken chain of our successes, both in skirmishes and general engagements, since the commencement of this (on our part) unavoidable war, that a mightier arm than that of Mars, would seem to have volunteered upon our side. At Mesilla, in Arizona, Lt. Colonel Baylor, with four companies of Texan recruits and a few citizens—numbering in all three hundred men—defeated eleven companies of six hundred United States regulars, compelling them to surrender Fort Fillmore, and taking possession of $500,000 worth of property; at Vienna, Col. Gregg's South Carolina regiment and a company of Virginia artillery, routed General Schenck's brigade, with a loss of one hundred and fifty men, but not one killed or wounded on our side; at Haynesville, Colonel Jackson, with two regiments, kept a comparatively immense army, under General Patterson, in check; at Greenbrier River, with a loss of nine on our side, General H. R. Jackson defeated a greatly superior force of the enemy under General Reynolds; at Chicamacomico, a Georgia regiment, commanded by Colonel Wright, chased an Indiana regiment twenty miles, and captured about forty prisoners; in the Passes of the Mississippi, Commodore Hollins, with a "Mosquito" fleet, put to flight a Federal blockading armada;

in Carthage, Missouri, General Price defeated, with
heavy loss, Siegel's army; at Lewinsville, several regiments of the enemy upon reconnoissance, were surprised
by Confederates; at Santa Rosa, General Anderson,
with five hundred Confederates, attacked Colonel Wilson—in days gone by, a kind of professional highway-
man, or midnight baggage-smasher—in his encampment,
put his whole command to flight, burned the camp, and
caused the distinguished Wilson to fly in an apparel ele-
gant as that which Adam wore before the Fall; recently
the contending forces met on equal terms at Belmont,
about 10,000 men on either side, yet the enemy were
driven back with terrible slaughter and decimation; at
Cross Lanes, Colonel Tyler's 7th Ohio regiment was
"cut to pieces" by a portion of General Floyd's command; at Hawk's Nest, one hundred Confederates put
to flight nearly six hundred Federals, with but four killed
and wounded on our side; at Guyandotte, Colonel Clark-
son, with a squadron of cavalry, dashed upon the enemy,
killed sixty and took one hundred and four prisoners,
without suffering on his side the loss of a single soul;
at Carnifax Ferry, General Floyd, with seventeen hundred Southerners, repulsed over four thousand Federals,
under General Rosencranz, who attempted to drive us
from our position—the latter losing not less than six
hundred, while our loss was but trifling; and finally, at
Leesburg, the 13th, 17th, and 19th Mississippi regiments, and the 8th Virginia regiment, numbering
twenty-five hundred men in all, met the 15th and 20th
Massachusetts regiments, the 42d New York and 1st
California, and portions of the 1st New Jersey, 40th
New York, 3rd Rhode Island, and a Pennsylvania cavalry—in all, more than four thousand men—defeated

them, took six hundred and eighty prisoners, and put nearly fourteen hundred others *hors de combat!*

In all this—aiding, guiding, protecting us—the Divine hand of Heavenly interposition has been manifested—the God of men and nations nerving and shielding the ranks of the just. In less than eight months, our Confederacy has had accessions of five sovereign States; embracing millions of souls, thousands of territorial square miles, and inexhaustible treasures; and ere eight months more are passed, three other States will, doubtless, have joined their fortunes to the Southern Empire. With signal success, the enemy has been met at almost every point; his ranks broken; his pride humbled with the dust; his vaunting columns routed in confusion and dismay; his malignity despised, derided, and defied; and his people brought to the thresholds of poverty, uncertainty, and despair. On our side, there are unanimity, power, patriotic integrity of purpose, patience under difficulties, resolution to conquer, and that dignity which springs from consciousness of strength. On his side are divided counsels, vacillation, chicanery, cowardice, ignorant numbers, and impotency in action. *We* have Generals of genius and military experience; wise and patriotic statesmen; and a citizen soldiery, armed to maintain their rights—defend their soil, homes, and firesides. *His* Generals are charlatans, pretenders, speculators; his forces, composed of hungry and shivering hirelings, enlisted to invade the sanctuaries of superiors, and compelled to do so only by terror of starvation. His people are idle and destitute, ours buoyant and prosperous. While we are husbanding our resources, he is barbarously squandering his. Enterprise, genius, and art, are impelled to move onward here; with him they are constrained to retrogress or remain stagnant. He wears the armor of Tyranny, while we bear the scales of Justice and wield the sword of Liberty. Our motives are—to preserve honor, freedom, independence, and win a place among the family of nations; his—to subjugate, chain, and rob us. Our acts, in this war, have been marked, so far, by leniency, humanity, civilization, and christianity; while his cruelties and fiendish atrocities, outwonder the devilisms of fiction, and fix a deep indentation of horror and disgrace upon the escutcheon of the century. And if we have erred, our sin has been in not properly appreciating the nature of the diabolical foe with whom we have had to contend. Judging him by our own subjectiveness and the conduct of other men, when in our power, after the battle of Manassas, instead of laying his fields in waste and giving his cities to the flames, we spared him and returned good for evil, hoping that he had learned wisdom, if not charity, by a too dearly purchased experience. But were we right in so supposing? Were we wise in conceiving that a foe, who, in peace, had been the prince of swindlers—who, to cheat the public, could stoop even to the low fraud of manufacturing wooden nutmegs—would be either generous or magnanimous in war? Milton and Göethe lived before this era, and, consequently, Satan and Mephistopheles, are imperfect impersonations of Evil—his devilship is here incarnadined: and as the mask is gradually removed, men avert their shuddering glance, from his face, as if withered by beholding the countenance of Eblis. He has resorted to every vile device and stratagem, which the powers of darkness could suggest; and crimes which the Genius of Poetry denied to the dark inventions of Wizard and Enchanter, are to our enemy of quick conception and easy delivery. He wages a relentless war upon women and children—robbing the widow of her mite and the orphan of death's legacy. He has put a blazing torch in the hand of incendiaries, humbling temples of prayer erected in praise of the living God, public institutes, and dwellings of rich and lowly, to one mass of common ruin. He has proposed the arming of servile hands for purposes of murder and wholesale slaughter; and with this view, he has entered into alliance with a semi-barbarous colony. While our prisons groan with his captives—some of them sick, wounded, and maimed—and while they at least number five times as many as those of our men in his hands, he is not only oblivious to the confinement, want, sufferings, anguish of soul and body, which those unfortunates who helped to fight his battles have necessarily to undergo—refusing to have, in accordance with the usages of civilized war, any portion of them exchanged; but he proposes to massacre in cold blood, the crew of one of our privateers, thereby inaugurating a policy, foreign and revolting to all except savages, and forcing our Government to adopt the law of Retaliation, which, however revolting to the susceptibilities of our people, must be inexorably and terribly enforced—no matter who may suffer on either side, or what the social or political stations of sufferers. Finally, and to crown his infamy, he has inaugurated a crime against mankind, present and prospective, by undertaking to perpetually blockade the principal inlets, ports, and harbors of the South, with useless and rejected vessels filled. with stones sunk in their harbors; and this he terms, in his satanic vocabulary, "the stone blockade."

And yet, the successes of this violent, ferocious, and

inhuman foe have been few and paltry—so few that they can be reckoned upon one's fingers—so paltry as not to be far removed from the ludicrous. Those which he achieved at Boonesville and Philippi, would not redound to the glory of Lilliputians. At St. George, it is true, the lamented General Garnett fell; and at Rich Mountain, thirteen hundred Federalists defeated two hundred and fifty of our troops and took Col. Pegram prisoner. A powerful fleet attacked and stormed a few of our sand batteries at Hatteras, an inlet upon the coast of North Carolina; but where, however, the enemy is welcome to remain, so long as his treasury, tastes, and the ocean will admit. The great fleet fitted out at the North, for the ravage of the South, at an expense of nearly five millions of dollars, resulted merely in the capture of Port Royal—a fruitless victory, since the cotton which they intended to steal or rob its owners of, was promptly given to the flames by the patriotism of those who had already given their best beloved to the service of their country. And in enumerating the achievements of the enemy, perhaps his forcible search of a British mail steamer, and his arrest upon her deck of our ambassadors—Messrs. Mason and Slidell—should not be omitted; but as this *victory* is at the expense of England's honor and pride, and as that nation has rarely tolerated international insult or outrage, it is not unlikely to prove to him bitter as Dead Sea fruit. But his final, signal, and characteristic victory, has been the recognition of Hayti—a victory whereby Lincoln has become the oldest brother of Giffrard—the Puritans have been wed to the *Vaudoux*—and the New England form of Christianity leagued with Haytien fetichism.

The people of our Confederacy have reason to rejoice

and give thanks, for the many important victories and
unexpected chain of successes, which have crowned their
arms; for the comparatively few and trifling reverses they
have experienced; for the great impulse of progress imparted to their industry, resources, and ingenuity—illustrating to them, for the first time, their own power; for
their undoubted prospects of being in future metropoli-
tans, instead of provincials—masters, in place of dependents—and teachers, where they were pupils; but, particularly, for their providential delivery from a continuance
of association with those who were their former allies,
and who are now their cruel, bloodthirsty, and abominable foes. Favored, as she is, with every element of
greatness and splendor, the position which Nature designed the South to occupy, is that of Empress of the
continent. Her people have the intellect and breeding
which qualify them to guide and rule, and they should
enforce their prerogative. She is producer of commodities upon which the welfare and happiness of a great
portion of mankind depend; and as the summer's sun
first visits her clime, and loves to linger there the
longest, so should her civilization be brilliant, genial,
and sublime. But let it not be overlooked or forgotten,
that a nation's independence has seldom been cheaply
won—the price of liberty is perpetual vigilance, sacrifice
of peace, precious blood, and costly treasures. The
South could not, even if she so desired, now recede from
the proud attitude which she has assumed. She must be
vassal, or free; her people shall be sovereign citizens, or
craven serfs; she must wear the queenly diadem, or sit
in the embers of slavery—a Cinderella among the nations. No goal of splendor is ever reached, without
adversities and misfortunes rendering the path toward it

rugged and uncertain—not even the ineffable happiness of the Elysium-life hereafter. Nor is *her* road to freedom and independence, in this dreadful contest, likely to be strewn with flowers. The best blood of her heroes may redden her soil; her daughters be compelled to wear sable weeds of sorrow; her young and helpless ones orphaned; her coasts pillaged and plundered; some of her cities devastated; and her harvest fields made desolate. But let her people buckle on the armor of fortitude, be patient and hopeful under difficulties, and unflinchingly resolute and determined in the hour of danger. For He who tested the fidelity and soothed the sorrows of Job—who levels the palace and the hovel, and replenishes the grave—who is the undying perfection of the living, and in whose hand are the universal . dominions—who tempers the wind to the shorn lamb, and comforted His servant in the lion's den—the God who delivered His people from Egyptian bondage, to whom the lightnings of heaven and shields of earth belong—was the God of our fathers, is our God— and doth He not defend us with the mighty ægis of His protection?

www.ingramcontent.com/pod-product-compliance
Lightning Source LLC
Chambersburg PA
CBHW020620030726
47497CB00007B/2342